THE TRAIL OF TRASK

Trask had ridden up into the high country after a deadly duel. Suddenly collapsing in agony, the gunfighter realized that he had been wounded. He tried in vain to reach his guns, hanging over the neck of his stallion. Lying helpless on the ground, he heard something in the forest coming towards him; it would not be the last thing to seek him out during the following twenty-four hours. Would he live to fight another day?

MICHAEL D. GEORGE

THE TRAIL OF TRASK

Complete and Unabridged

LINFORD
Leicester

First published in Great Britain in 2005 by
Robert Hale Limited
London

First Linford Edition
published 2006
by arrangement with
Robert Hale Limited
London

British Library CIP Data

George, Michael D.
  The trail of Trask.—Large print ed.—
  Linford western library
  1. Western stories
  2. Large type books
  I. Title
  823.9'14 [F]

  ISBN 1–84617–319–1

Published by
F. A. Thorpe (Publishing)
Anstey, Leicestershire

Set by Words & Graphics Ltd.
Anstey, Leicestershire
Printed and bound in Great Britain by
T. J. International Ltd., Padstow, Cornwall

This book is printed on acid-free paper

745600)

*Dedicated with gratitude and love
to my youngest son
Denis Roy Michael George*

Prologue

The outlaw was lifted off his feet by the sheer force of the two well placed bullets. He was then thrown ten feet backwards and crashed on to the dried centre of the hotel hitching rail. The pole snapped. The lifeless body landed in the dust. Acrid smoke still drifted and swirled in the dry air from the hot barrels of the twin guns towards the stunned and startled onlookers who watched silently from both sides of the wide main street. Yet the silver-haired man that had become known throughout the West simply as Trask seemed to know little of the deadly justice he had just administered.

His head had remained lowered throughout the showdown with Denver Ben Davis. It was as if he had not even aimed the deadly weapons he held.

For unlike any other gunfighter who

roamed the vast untamed lands west of the Pecos, Trask had never seemed able to accept the fact that he was unmatched with his deadly weaponry. He simply could not accept that it was he who was responsible for the decades of unrivalled showdowns.

Trask believed that there was some unseen power in the actual guns themselves. A power which had entrapped his very soul to do their handiwork for nearly thirty long trail-weary years. It was not he who was the master of the gun skills, Trask believed. He was merely their servant.

For most gunmen who found the perfect guns and learned how to deal out their venomous lead always boasted that it was their skill which made them better than their adversaries.

Trask however had never once considered himself a master of the smoking guns he held in his shaking hands as he turned back towards his faithful horse. For they had become a curse that he feared he would never be able to shake off. He was old now and had lived in the shadow of his strange handsome guns since he had first walked into manhood. That fateful day when his skin was still fresh and hair gleamed as only youngsters' hair can gleam still haunted him.

For he had not been Trask then.

The name had been branded on to the handtooled gunbelt he had found in the store. He had been entranced by the pair of mother-of-pearl-handled silver-plated Eagle-Butt Peace-maker .45s with their intricate design of an eagle fighting a rattler and seven-inch barrels, as they hung in the hardware-store window. It might have been the way the morning sun had danced along their highly polished surfaces that had first lured him. Whatever it was, from that moment on he had only one thought in his then youthful mind.

He had to possess them.

Even though it had taken every cent of his meagre savings he had willingly purchased the guns and their fancy shooting-rig. From that day on he had become known by the name branded on the gunbelt.

Trask!

Trask had never once failed to draw his guns more speedily than his enemies. Never once had his guns failed to spew deadly lead from their long seven-inch barrels before his opponents' guns had even cleared their holsters.

His guns had always allowed Trask to defend the weak against the evil that had spread across the Pecos like a cancerous sore; to administer justice where it was required.

Few men ever become legends in their own lifetimes, but Trask had achieved that goal without even trying. His fame as a gunfighter grew with every passing day. Until the days had stretched out into years and then decades.

But even legends grow old.

The tall man known for so long as Trask became more and more convinced in his belief that it was not he, but the guns themselves that were blessed or cursed to never be defeated in combat.

Never to miss their chosen target.

How could he have always managed to outdraw the best gunslingers who had faced him down? Could it have been luck or something else? Trask knew that it simply did not make any sense.

If it was the guns that possessed the power, then he was just the present servant of the mysterious weaponry.

He was just the present Trask. There must have been others who had also been known by the name that was emblazoned on the leather of the broad belt. Others who had been slaves to the guns that never once failed the man who strapped their shooting-rig around his hips. Perhaps the others had become old, as he had, and died in their sleep. The guns then waited for the next willing and able man to adopt them. Or had they faced one gunslinger too many?

It seemed a loco idea, even to Trask, but he knew the power of the pair of guns he slowly dropped back into the well-used holsters.

They could find his hands long before he realized that there was trouble brewing. Never once had they missed their target in all the years he had been their guardian.

Yet he was now tired.

Tired of the killing. Exhausted from the relentless trail he had ridden for most of his life. He had outlived five sturdy horses in his vain quest for answers to questions that burned into his very soul like branding-irons.

But there were no answers, simply more trail to ride.

Once the carefree existence of a drifter had seemed perfect to the man who had his entire life before him.

Now he felt that he was living on borrowed time.

He had found fear riding on his shoulder during the past few years. Fear that the guns would one day decide they wanted a new man to wield their awesome power.

Every sinew in his lean frame ached as age began to take its inevitable toll. Just getting up off the hard ground each morning was becoming more and more of an effort. The camp-fires no longer warmed his bones as they had once done.

He had searched vainly for a place where he could rest. A place where he would no longer have to use the guns. The search had become the only spur which kept him riding on and on. There had to be a peaceful place somewhere.

It was a weary Trask who unbuckled the belt and hung it over the neck of his chestnut stallion. He looked back over his shoulder at the pale faces of the townsfolk who had witnessed the deadly duel which had ended only two minutes earlier.

None of the men and women uttered a word as he held on to the saddle horn and raised his left boot up until it slid into the leather stirrup. They watched in awe as he mounted the stallion and turned its head away from the long hitching pole. Even the sheriff remained in his office staring through the open window from behind his desk as the horse walked towards the forested trail.

Every one of the wide-eyed onlookers knew that they had just witnessed one of the last of the living legends dealing out justice to vermin in human form. Vermin that had had the run of their town until Trask had ridden into their midst.

There had been countless others like Denver Ben Davis. Trask had defeated them all and never once capitalized on his victories.

The crowd were still silent as he rode slowly between them and headed back into the high country.

Trask felt a bead of sweat trace its way across his wrinkled features and drip on to the once expensive shirt, which now resembled a frayed rag to the onlookers. None who had heard the name of Trask over the countless years had imagined that they would ever set eyes upon him or that he would look the way he did. Legends are meant to be almost like gods. But the aged rider who spoke only when spoken to looked nothing like a god. He was an old man and yet still the fastest draw in the West. The speed of his hands defied the power of any of them to focus on the actual deed he had so swiftly executed. None had ever seen a man draw and fire so effortlessly before.

As he tapped his spurs into the flesh of his mount he knew that their eyes were not aimed at him.

They were staring at the gleaming holstered guns hanging over the saddle horn.

His guns. The guns of Trask.

1

The high country was cold. So cold it froze the air that came from the horse's and rider's mouths into clouds of mist as they continued to ascend the mountain. The sun was low and filtered through the endless trees which surrounded the narrow dusty trail. But there was no heat in it.

An eerie light danced on the rays of sunshine which managed to force their way through the straight, thin pines. Yet Trask did not notice anything except the pearl-handled gun-grips before him. His left hand gripped the saddle horn as his right held on to his reins.

Trask continued on up through the freezing air and the trees that fringed the narrow trail. The gunfighter had no idea where the trail would lead him. All he had ever done was continue his vain quest for peace and never to retrace his own trail.

His stallion was exhausted and yet would not quit until its master eased back on the long reins. It would continue on until its heart burst, if that was what Trask wanted.

Trask had ridden more than a score of miles through the sea of tall trees before he noticed the blood on his pants'-leg in the last rays of the dying sun. He rubbed his eyes and stared hard at the dark mark he had not noticed before.

It suddenly dawned on him that this was his blood and that he had lost a heap of it.

He dragged back on his reins and stopped the horse. He tried to clear his mind but his brain was numbed by the cold and the loss of so much blood. For what felt like an eternity Trask stared down at the dark evidence of his injury. He then searched for the wound itself.

It did not take long to locate.

Trask felt the sharp agonizing pain rip through him as his gloved fingers located the bullet hole a few inches above his left hip. There was another hole a few inches around his thin waist where the bullet had left his lean body.

'Darn it!' Trask growled. 'Denver Ben shot me!'

The gunfighter had not even noticed that he had been wounded until now. A mixture of frayed nerves and the ice-cold mountain air had numbed him.

He slowly dismounted the tall stallion, looped the reins around a tall, thin sapling and secured them well. He then studied the brush around him. It was dense. Trask knew that it was not wise for any wounded creature to remain too long in the high country with so much hungry game desperate for a meal.

A million unseen hunters lived in the forested mountains waiting to catch the scent of fresh, easy prey.

The wounded man looked at the sunlight that traced across the countless tree trunks. It was getting fainter with every beat of his pounding heart.

The trail ahead was vague and

seemed to lead nowhere except in and out of the trees. He knew that he would not find shelter before the sun eventually set.

Trask shook his head but his thoughts grew no sharper.

Soon it would be dark and he knew that even the light of a full moon could never penetrate the thick canopy fifty or more feet above him. If he had not felt so weak, he might have been worried. But Trask did not have the strength to be worried. His hands found his canteen and unscrewed its stopper. He drank and then poured what was left over his face in an attempt to wake up his dwindling senses. He felt no better as he hung the canteen back on his saddle horn next to his gunbelt.

Then he heard a faint sound. He managed to straighten up and look in the direction from whence it had come. Even in his weakened condition, he was still curious.

Trask had started to move away from his mount towards the closest bushes when he felt giddy. He staggered. Then his legs buckled beneath him.

He was falling.

Trask hit the ground hard; so hard that he felt every last ounce of wind being kicked out of his lean frame. As he rolled over on to his back, he saw the almost orange rays of the setting sun streaming through the canopy of branches and leaves above him.

Pain burned like a branding-iron through him. It rushed like quicksilver and found every nerve in his body.

Trask screamed out and then it was gone. He heard himself pant like an old hound-dog whilst beads of sweat ran down his face and burned his eyes.

His confused mind tried to make sense of a stampede of thoughts.

Had he allowed the countless hours of loneliness as he drifted from one lethal encounter after another, to convince him of something which was impossible?

The guns were mere guns! No more!

He lay on the ground, trying to get

back up, when he felt his side start to hurt. Trask tilted his head and tried to see the pain that racked his body.

Blood started to flow more freely from his wound.

'This ain't good!' he muttered as he pushed his gloved hand on to the wound. 'Nope, this ain't good at all.'

He tried to get back up off the ground, but it was as if he were nailed there.

'Darn it!' he cursed. 'I'm just an old fool. Weak as a kitten after just one hole in my side.'

Then another noise caught his attention. It sounded closer than before.

'The way my luck's been panning out today, that's gotta be a puma!' Trask turned his head and screwed up his eyes until they were locked on to the direction where he could hear the noise.

It was a rider, he thought.

But who was it?

Another challenger who wanted to

face the invincible Trask?

Another young pretender wishing to become crowned as the fastest gun in the West? Maybe Denver Ben had kinfolk back in town.

Trask then heard another sound behind him. He tried to turn his head again but could not.

He listened to the second noise.

What was it?

Certainly not a rider like the first. Whatever it was, it was on foot. Either two or four, but approaching him fast. Too darn fast.

The sound of bone-dry kindling snapping underfoot alerted Trask. His hands moved to his hips and vainly searched for the trusty gun-grips.

Then Trask focused his eyes on the gunbelt hanging over the neck of his stallion. Sweat began to drip even more freely over his weathered features. The guns could not help him now. For the first time in thirty years, he was helpless.

The brush began to move as

someone or something moved through it toward him.

He could hear the sound of the horse's breath as its master forced it through the bushes towards him.

'I hear ya!' Trask yelled out. 'Whoever you are, I can hear ya.'

There was no reply.

2

Trask was in trouble and knew it. He lay helplessly on the hard unforgiving ground, desperately trying to hear above the sound of his pounding heart. They were still approaching from both sides but he could do nothing to stop them. Trask kept staring at his gunbelt hanging over the neck of his stallion. For the first time in three decades, he realized how valuable they were to him.

The sun had sunk fast during the seemingly endless few minutes since he had first detected the sound of unseen visitors to either side of him.

Trask inhaled deeply and awaited his fate.

The bushes to his right moved again and a small well-built grey horse pushed its way into the clearing before being reined in. Trask gritted his teeth and stared through the half-light at the bearded rider. He had never set eyes upon a man quite so hairy before. A coonskin cap sat atop a mane of long unkempt hair and merged into a beard.

Two small fiery eyes glinted in the dying rays of the setting sun. Trask swallowed hard as he studied the strange horseman more closely.

The man's entire clothing appeared to be made of bearskin or the pelt of some similar forest creature that the gunfighter had probably never even heard of. The horse beneath the rider was also covered in long shaggy hair. Trask shivered and knew that whoever this man was, he was dressed for the climate, unlike himself.

This was a mountain man!

The horseman pulled back on his reins again and stared long and hard down at the prostrate Trask. If there was any emotion in the mountain man's features, the gunfighter was unable to detect it amid all the hair and fur.

The man eased himself to his left and

then dragged a long rifle from its scabbard beneath his saddle. It was unlike any rifle the gunfighter had ever seen.

The weapon was like Trask himself. It was a relic of a bygone time. It was a buffalo gun.

Trask swallowed hard and watched the rider slide a large-calibre bullet into its solitary chamber. A gloved thumb hauled the massive hammer back until it clicked loudly.

The horseman then raised the rifle up until its stock was resting in the crook of his shoulder. He stared down the long barrel and aimed it in Trask's direction.

Again Trask swallowed hard.

He opened his mouth to speak to the hairy horseman when the rider shook his head. Trask's attention was then drawn to the sound behind him.

Bushes could be heard as they were ripped apart.

Again Trask tried to turn and see what was coming at him through the dark mass of trees and brushes. He felt himself fall on to his back as his energy drained from him. Whatever it was that was crashing its way through the brush towards him, it had to be big. Darn big.

His eyes darted back at the mountain man.

The rider was standing in his stirrups with one eye closed tightly. He was staring down the entire length of the long barrel as he trained it on the brush behind Trask.

Trask watched the steam of his breath increase its pace from his open mouth. His heart felt like an Apache war drum inside his heaving chest.

Suddenly there was a sound like nothing Trask had ever heard before. A roar that almost burst his eardrums. He could feel the ground beneath him shake under the weight of whatever it was that had just broken out from the brush.

Another deafening noise echoed all around the clearing.

Trask looked at the mountain man,

who remained upright in his stirrups holding on to his trusty rifle. The grey horse seemed to be so well-trained that it remained perfectly still even though the fierce growling grew louder and more terrifying.

Trask's own stallion was a different matter. It was wide-eyed and feverishly trying to break free of its restraints.

Then the rider squeezed on his trigger.

No stick of dynamite could have equalled the deafening sound.

Trask turned his face away as he saw the rifle barrel of the mountain man spew out its massive charge. Smoke billowed in a huge circle around the rider as his deadly bullet erupted across the clearing just above the helpless gunfighter's body.

It was like a thunderclap. Then there was a sickening noise just behind Trask.

He had heard it before many times.

It was the sound of death.

The ground stopped shaking for a brief moment and then he felt it shudder as the impact of the unseen creature landed right behind him.

The mountain man eased himself off his grey and walked slowly toward Trask. Within two strides, he had discharged the smoking bullet-casing and reloaded.

Trask watched silently as the bearded man got closer and closer to him. The rifle jutted out from hip level and was aimed at whatever it was behind the legendary gunfighter.

The man stepped over Trask as if he were not even there and continued on until he reached his stricken prey.

'Ya can start breathin' again, dude,' the mountain man called out from behind Trask. 'This varmint is good and dead.'

Trask managed to ease himself on to his side and stared in disbelief at the sight which met his eyes in the fading light.

He had never seen anything so large before.

The massive black bear lay in a pool

of its own blood as the mountain man paced around its body.

'A bear!' Trask sighed.

'Sure it's a bear.' The man snorted. 'What ya think it was? A racoon or somethin'?'

Trask watched the man lower his rifle and walk back to him. He stared up and could only see the hint of a nose and two sparkling eyes amid the fur and hair.

'Why did that critter attack, stranger?' Trask asked.

'He smelled ya blood,' came the sharp reply. 'To him you was an easy supper. Lucky for you that me and old Curly there caught ya scent when we did.'

'Curly?' Trask repeated the name.

'My hoss Curly, old man.' The man shook his head in disgust. 'You ain't very bright, is ya?'

Trask smiled through his pain.

'Not at the moment, I ain't. If I was smart I'd not be bleeding all over myself.'

The man knelt, peeled back the blood-soaked shirt and looked down at the injury. He seemed unimpressed.

'I've seen worse. I'll fix ya wound for ya.'

'That's mighty kind of you, stranger.' Trask licked his dry lips.

'Ain't kindness. Gotta stop ya bleeding before the smell of ya blood brings every darn mountain lion down on our necks,' the man said. 'And my name ain't stranger, it's Waldo. Waldo Zane.'

Trask blinked hard.

'What about the blood of that bear, Waldo? Surely that'll bring the whole damn forest down on us too!'

'Bear blood don't taste good to any of the forest critters. I heard tell that if'n ya eats the innards of a bear, it'll kill ya faster than poison.' Waldo shrugged. 'I'll skin him in the morning before we heads out.'

'Where we going?'

'Ain't figured that far ahead yet. It'll come to me, though,' the mountain man admitted as he rose back to his full height. He looked down on the weak gunfighter. 'Say, have you gotta name?'

'They call me Trask.'

'What ya mean by that?' Waldo scratched his sides. 'Ya say that they call ya Trask? I don't understand.'

'It's a long story, Waldo.' Trask smiled.

'Damn stupid name if ya asks me. Reckon it suits ya though.' Waldo rested his rifle down beside the gunfighter and started to gather up kindling, piling it a few feet away from Trask's boots. 'Ya don't look too bright. Reckon ya must be a little loco. To ride up here dressed like that with a hole in ya. If Trask means dumb, ya got the right handle there, old man.'

If Trask had not felt so weak, he might have been able to laugh. But all he could do was watch as the pile of wood grew larger until the mountain man covered it with dry moss and then struck a match along the edge of his left boot. He cupped the flame and then tossed it into the pyramid of kindling.

The flames leapt upward and immediately illuminated the clearing. Waldo
continued to pile larger and larger
branches on top of the flames until he
was satisfied that it would continue
burning unhindered through the night.

'Ya hungry, Trask?'

The veteran gunfighter felt the pain
rip through him as the warmth of the
camp-fire allowed his body to thaw.
Trask buckled over and felt his face
bury itself in the grass beside him.

Waldo moved swiftly for a giant.

He plucked Trask off the ground as if
he weighed no more than a child. The
mountain man turned and then saw a
flat area near the fire. He strode to the
spot and gently lowered Trask down
before pulling the blood-soaked shirt
away from the horrific wound.

Trask could not understand what was
happening to him. For the first time
since he had ridden away from the
small town, hours earlier, he felt as if
his mind was filled with fog.

Waldo Zane pulled a long-bladed

knife from his belt and rested its blade in the hot flames beside him.

'Reckon the meal will have to wait until I've fixed ya up.' He rose up and moved to his grey horse. His large fingers searched in his saddlebags until they located what they sought.

He returned to the delirious Trask and dropped beside him the half-full bottle of whiskey and roll of catgut with a large sewing-needle rammed into it. Waldo's eyes then scanned the trees that surrounded them until he located the small willow fighting for survival between so many pines.

The large man forged his way through the brush and rested his huge hands on the trunk of the willow. His fingers clawed at the bark until he managed to pull a chunk of it off. He then returned to the fire and knelt beside Trask.

'By the sound of that gibberish ya talkin', Trask, I'd better get workin' on ya fast.' Waldo rammed the tree-bark between the teeth of the ailing man.

'Suck on that. Chew it if'n ya want. It'll help kill the pain.'

The gunfighter's eyes were glazed as Waldo pushed the bark between his teeth.

Trask did not feel the red-hot knife-blade as it cleaned the edge of the wound. Trask never even felt the whiskey as it was poured over the still bleeding wound.

The mountain man then threaded the large needle after he had heated it up in the smouldering ashes of the fire beside him.

'Good job ya loco right now, old-timer,' Waldo said as he thrust the sharp needle into Trask's flesh and started to sew up the bleeding bullet hole. 'And if'n ya knew that I only ever sewed up leather before, I reckon ya would be a tad troubled.'

Trask could hear the muffled words above him but there was no understanding. He then sank into the deepest sleep he had ever known.

A sleep which, if he were lucky, he would return from.

3

Hickory Creek was one of the most remote towns in all of the high country in the north of Montana. It had blazing-hot summers and freezing-cold winters. It had always been the harshness of the winter months which had slowed its progress. For no matter how many people found their way to the small town during the summer, few remained once the weather started to turn. The few who did remain were those who had faced a lot worse than ice and snow in their lifetimes, or men such as Denver Ben Davis, with a price on their heads. Men who needed to disappear for a while in order to get the law off their backs. Hickory Creek was starting to feel the first signs of the impending winter weather as its streets echoed to the beat of a horse's hoofs.

It was three minutes after midnight

by the clock on the wall of the sheriff's office when the sound of a cantering horse drew the veteran lawman's attention from the pile of wanted posters set out before him on his cluttered desk.

Sheriff Barney Cole rose up from his chair, leaned forward and blew down the blackened glass lamp-funnel until the flame extinguished on the wick. He then straightened up and felt the sweat trickle down his whiskered face from his crop of white hair. The sight of Trask standing in the middle of the main street facing the well-tailored Davis still burned into his mind. In all his days as a lawman, he had never once witnessed anything like the deadly showdown before. Trask had done what no other man in Hickory Creek had been willing or able to do. And then, without even bothering to collect the reward money, he had ridden off in the direction of the trees. Cole had good reason to be troubled as he rested the palm of his left hand on the wooden window-frame for he knew that there were more than one Davis in these parts. He cautiously stared out of the office's large window.

His eyes narrowed and watched as the solitary rider drove his lathered-up mount down the centre of the main street towards the brightly lit saloon.

Cole rubbed his face and wiped the sweat off his hand on to his chequered shirt. He recognized the horseman as he dismounted and walked into the well-illuminated saloon.

It was Pate Davis. Denver Ben's younger, more unpredictable brother. Not a fancy dresser like Denver Ben, but far more vicious and dangerous. Cole had seen the younger Davis pistol-whip and kill for little or no reason since the pair had moved into the town. Yet he had been helpless to do a thing as it was always self-defence. Even the most law-abiding of townsfolk would agree with Pate Davis when he asked if his victim had been the first to go for his gun.

Sheriff Cole knew that he had to face his own fears as well the deadly guns of the volatile outlaw before Davis heard the news of his brother's fate from the drunken lips of someone within the saloon. There was no telling how many people might eat lead if Pate took the news of Denver Ben's death badly.

He pulled his gunbelt off the hatstand and strapped it around his middle, picked up his shotgun and checked that both its barrels were loaded with buckshot.

Cole steadied himself and then opened the office door and stepped out on to the porch. He knew that Pate Davis, unlike Denver Ben, had a mean streak that bordered on the insane. Without the older Denver Ben to calm him down, there was no telling what the young outlaw would do.

Pate had already added a couple of notches to his gun grip since the brothers had first ridden into the normally quiet town, and there would have been a lot more if not for Denver Ben.

Cole stepped down into the street and cautiously made his way towards the lathered-up mount and the strangely silent saloon. The lawman had heard the tinny piano stop playing as soon as Davis entered.

Now the customers were drifting hurriedly out of the saloon and heading for cover. Even the dance-hall girls could be seen making their way far more quickly than was their usual style.

Barney Cole stepped up on to the boardwalk and inhaled deeply as if he were trying to drag courage from the cool night air before he entered the saloon.

The swing-doors were flapping as the veteran lawman walked slowly into the brightly lit saloon. He stopped and looked around the now almost empty drinking-hole. He swallowed hard.

Pate Davis was pouring himself a whiskey at the bar.

'What in tarnation is going on here?' Davis asked the nervous bartender. 'Have I got the plague or somethin'?'

The bartender forced a smile and continued drying glasses as he watched Cole moving towards them with the shotgun across his chest.

Davis turned his head, then tossed the whiskey down his dry throat before he poured another. He nodded at the lawman and then returned his attention back to the bartender.

'Ya seen Denver Ben tonight?'

The bartender gulped.

'I . . . I . . . don't really know, Pate.'

'What kinda answer is that?' Davis lowered the glass and rested it on the wet surface of the bar counter. His eyes then focused in the mirror behind the bartender on the sheriff, who was now at his left elbow.

'I got some bad news for ya, Pate,' Cole said.

Davis did not bother to turn his head. He continued to watch the lawman's reflection.

'I never seen you look so serious before, Cole.'

'Denver Ben is dead, son,' the sheriff muttered.

Davis turned and looked at the older man. There was total confusion in the outlaw's expression.

'Denver Ben? Dead?'

'Yep.'

Suddenly the look altered and Davis's eyes narrowed until they became mere slits. His teeth gritted and he started to snarl like a wild animal.

'You kill my brother? Did ya?' Davis shouted as his every sinew shook until he could not control his anger.

The open-mouthed bartender watched in horror as Davis dragged the shotgun from Cole's hands and tossed it across the saloon. Then he grabbed the lawman and lifted him off his feet.

'Let go of me, Pate!' Cole demanded.

'Ya kill him? Back-shoot him? Did ya? Did ya?'

Sheriff Cole tried to reply but Davis had moved his left hand from his shirt collar and encircled his throat with his long powerful fingers. Then he felt the cold steel barrel of the Colt push into his face.

'I oughta blow ya head clean off!' Davis yelled.

'It weren't him, Pate,' the bartender called out. 'It was the stranger.'

Pate Davis turned his head, released his grip and ignored the sheriff as he staggered backwards.

'What stranger?'

'Trask. They called him Trask,' the bartender stammered.

Pate Davis holstered his gun and rested both his hands on the bar counter.

'I heard of him a long time back. I thought he was dead. He killed Denver Ben?'

The bartender nodded.

'Yep. They had a showdown and — '

'Nobody ever outdrew Ben,' Davis protested.

Cole grunted his way to the bar, grabbed the whiskey-bottle and took a long swallow from its neck. He slammed it down and looked at the outlaw hard.

'Trask did, Pate. None of us ever seen such speed. It was like magic.'

'Trask? But I heard tales of him when I was a little kid. It must be a different varmint. He must be darn old by now.' Davis pulled the bottle from the lawman's hands and refilled his glass.

'He *is* old. Darn old. But still the fastest gun I ever done seen.'

Davis threw the whiskey down his throat.

'He ain't gonna get much older. Not when I catch up with him.'

4

A hundred war drums could not have sounded louder inside the pounding skull of Trask as at last he found himself awaking from the delirium which had overwhelmed him. The veteran gunfighter's eyelids flickered, sending red-hot pokers of pain burning up into his brain. Reluctantly, his wrinkled eyes opened and stared at the wall of flames that faced him.

For what seemed an eternity, Trask studied the well-fuelled camp-fire that roared upward into the blackness. Its flames twisted and licked the sky far above. The confused mind of the gunfighter wondered if he had finally arrived in Hell.

Then it dawned on him that if he were dead, the pain would have ended. Trask started to move when another barrel of gunpowder exploded inside his skull. He gave up the attempt and remained still.

For a few seemingly endless moments, Trask tried to work out where he was and what had happened. Slowly it all came back to him. The showdown, the wound that he had not even realized he had suffered until it was nearly too late. The bear and the huge mountain man.

'So ya ain't dead after all. Damn it. I was gonna skin ya and make me a new saddle out of ya worthless hide.' Waldo Zane's voice boomed as all huge men's voices do.

Trask managed to turn his head and looked at the kneeling mountain man, who was fixing something which almost resembled food in a huge skillet over the hot ashes.

'Waldo?'

'Yep. It's still me. Hope ya wasn't expectin' somebody else, Trask.' The mountain man stirred the sizzling food with the blade of the long knife. 'How'd ya feel? I only ask 'coz ya looks damn awful. I thought I'd done for ya.'

'My head hurts like thunder,' Trask replied quietly.

'It's ya own fault, old man.' Waldo sighed. 'I told ya to chew on that willow-bark. Ya stopped chewin' and kinda passed out when I was cleaning up ya bullet holes. Ain't my fault ya stopped chewin'. I told ya that bark would kill the pain.'

'Why would I chew on a lump of bark?' Trask tried to gather his thoughts. It was difficult. He could not recall anything after he had seen Zane kill the bear.

'Old Injun trick. It kills pain darn good.'

'How?'

'Do I look like an Injun?' the giant asked as he tipped the contents of the pan on to a pair of tin plates at his feet. 'I ain't got no idea how it stops the pain, all I know is that it does. OK?'

Trask was too weary to argue.

'OK.'

'I'd better get ya up so's ya can eat.'

The mountain man stood and then dropped the skillet on the ground behind him. He leaned over, grabbed Trask's wrists and dragged at the gunfighter until he was sitting upright. 'Ya ready for some vittles?'

'I ain't too hungry.' Trask winced as he felt his bones attempting to find their correct place inside his skin. 'All I want to do is sleep.'

'NO. No. No. Ya can't sleep, Trask!' Waldo said firmly. 'Ya might die of the lung fever. I seen it a dozen times. Folks with just a little bullet hole in 'em lying down. Then their lungs fills up. Nope, it's best that ya stays awake and eats.'

'Yeah?' Trask was even more confused.

'Honest. I ain't joshin' none.'

'I believe you, big man.'

Waldo picked up one of the plates and rammed it into the hands of the still groggy man.

'Eat or I'll get darn angry. I cooked double rations here and I can't stand to waste grub. Eat!'

Trask stared at the food on his plate. It was fried and yet did not appear to resemble anything he had ever seen or eaten before. He sniffed its unfamiliar aroma and then looked back at the huge bearded face.

'It sure looks good, Waldo,' Trask lied.

Suddenly there was a smile on the face of Waldo Zane. At least that was what Trask imagined it was. For a few teeth could be seen amid the massive unkempt beard and the eyes wrinkled up at their edges.

'Here. Have a spoon,' Waldo said, ramming a spoon on to the plate of the gunfighter. 'Don't use the things myself but I always keep one in case of company.'

'Thanks.' Trask stirred the food with the spoon. No amount of investigation made the meal's contents any clearer, though. He decided to change the subject. 'Tell me, Waldo, did ya manage to sew me up OK?'

'Sure. I used my best stitchin' too. I

kinda only use that when I'm doin' something fancy. Like a fixin' a belt.'

'I reckon I should be honoured.'

'Damn right, old-timer.' Waldo plucked his own plate up and started to eat with his fingers. He grunted with pleasure at every morsel that entered his well-hidden mouth. 'Bet ya ain't got no idea what this is, Trask.'

Trask blinked hard and then filled his spoon and raised it toward his own lips.

'Rabbit?'

'Ain't no rabbits around here, old-timer.' Waldo chewed heartily. 'Guess again.'

'I gotta admit it. I ain't got me no idea what this is.'

'Stew. Squirrel stew.'

Trask took the spoon in his mouth and started to eat. To his surprise, it tasted far better than it looked. He managed to swallow and then looked at Waldo licking his plate clean.

'Squirrel tastes pretty good.'

The mountain man nodded.

'Darn right it does. I could eat me a

dozen squirrels in one go. But they're real hard to catch, ya know.'

Trask took another mouthful and slowly chewed.

'Tasty. How come they're hard to catch?'

Waldo tossed his plate aside and then picked up the blackened coffee-pot off the fire. It was as if his huge hands did not feel the heat of the metal handle.

'They got the habit of running up trees. They're real fast little varmints. Have ya seen how far up these damn trees go?'

Trask continued eating.

'Reckon that buffalo gun of yours ain't much use with squirrels.'

The mountain man laughed. It was the loudest laugh the veteran gunfighter had ever heard. It seemed to ring out around the clearing.

'Ya feelin' a little better now, old-timer?'

Trask scooped the last of the food up off his plate and consumed it quickly. He then allowed his head to fall back against a tree-stump.

'You're sure a good host, Waldo. I feel a lot better now after eating that grub.'

The mountain man eyes sparkled in the firelight as he turned his head and looked at the gunfighter.

'I'm mighty pleased about that, Trask. For a while there I really thought ya was gonna die.'

Trask grinned.

'Looks like ya stuck with me now.'

Before Zane could say another word, there was a noise off in the distance which drew his attention. The massive man raised one of his huge hands as if to silence Trask. He then sighed and shook his head.

'What's wrong?' Trask asked.

'Injuns,' Waldo answered in a low tone that almost sounded like a growl.

Trask narrowed his eyes and felt his mouth suddenly go dry.

'Are they hostile in these parts?'

Waldo shook a tin cup. Dust floated into the flames.

'Never used to be. I heard tell that a

lotta tribes got themselves kicked off their lands down south. The last couple of years more and more of the critters have been giving me and the rest of my kind a whole heap of grief. They even tussle with the Injuns who have been up in these mountains for ever. I ain't even sure what tribes they are. But most of them are darn nasty and got a lotta hate for us.'

The gunfighter felt nervous. 'Would they attack us?'

Waldo shrugged.

'Depends. Ya can't say for certain one way or the other any more. But don't you go worryin' none and bustin' them stitches. They're a few miles away. Ain't no way they could get here before dawn. By then, we'll be long gone.'

Trask glanced at his horse and the gunbelt which still hung over its broad shoulders.

'Reckon you could get me my guns later, Waldo? I feel kinda naked without them.'

'Sure, but first drink this.' Waldo

poured out a cup of coffee and handed it to the wounded man.

'Thanks.'

'Gets lonely up here,' the mountain man said as his eyes stared into the flames of the fire. 'Nice to have someone to talk with. Curly is OK, but he ain't much of a talker.'

Trask blew into the tin cup.

'Curly?'

'My hoss!'

The gunfighter nodded slowly. He glanced at both their horses tied together close to the fire.

'I reckon I ain't much of a talker but I can talk a tad better than most horses.'

The mountain man laughed into his own cup.

'Only just, Trask. Only just.'

5

Gunsmoke trailed from the barrels of both the Remingtons as the outlaw watched the faces of his chosen volunteers. He twirled the guns, sending them back into their holsters. The five men now knew that he was deadly serious. They would ride with him or end up face first on the sawdust-covered saloon floor. Nobody ever refused Pate Davis when he ordered them to do anything. The outlaw rested his wrists on the wooden gun grips that jutted from his holsters and stared around the room. The sound of his shots still echoed in the men's ears.

Davis had a way about him which froze the blood in most men's souls. Some said it was the way his eyes burned into you as his low drawl muttered each carefully chosen word to make it sound like a threat. Others just knew that men like Pate Davis were never more than a few seconds away from unleashing their insanity with the deadly pair of Remingtons he was never seen without.

Whatever the reason, even law-abiding men tended to agree with anything the outlaw said. Perhaps most men never liked to think too much about their ultimate fate, hoping or praying that it would remain somewhere off in the distant future.

To face Pate Davis was a reminder that he could bring that day forward with horrifying brutality.

Davis sat down at a card-table and poured another tall whiskey. He tossed it into his mouth and swilled it around his teeth before swallowing.

The five men who surrounded the outlaw as he reached half-way down the whiskey-bottle were no outlaws, or even gunfighters like himself. They were just men who had witnessed the unnerving accuracy of his skills with his weaponry and wanted to live a little longer, and knew that agreeing with Davis might buy them a tad more time.

He had enlisted them to ride with him. There was no way that any of them would defy him.

Davis lifted his right leg and rested its spur on the green baize of the card-table. He eased his butt on the hard chair and looked at the faces around him: five men who were shaking so much that they could not do anything except stand watching the brooding outlaw.

Sheriff Barney Cole had not moved one inch along the wet bar since he had announced the news of Denver Ben's fate. He stood watching, as all wise men tend to do. He watched and listened and tried to fathom what he ought to do next.

Cole knew that Davis was like a stick of dynamite with its fuse already lit. When would it explode? And how many casualties would there be? It troubled the lawman.

The bartender knew that he should

have closed the saloon two hours earlier but he remained beside the mountain of stacked thimble-glasses, plying Davis and his five terrified cohorts with hard liquor. Like the other men in the saloon, he wanted to live long enough to see another dawn.

'Ya look like ya swallowed a chunk of tumbleweed, Sheriff,' Davis said as he swirled another three fingers of whiskey around in the glass.

Cole inhaled.

'Just thinkin', Pate. Just thinkin' about you and these yella-spined boys ya rounded up. Seems to me like ya picked a whole bunch of runts.'

Pate Davis tilted his head and poured the whiskey into his mouth. He swallowed and then returned his attention to the lawman.

'This is my posse, Cole.'

The lawman grunted with subdued laughter.

'Posse? That bunch of drunks?'

'Yep. I've sworn them in. They're my posse and we're gonna go find Trask and string the critter up. Reckon old Denver Ben would have liked that.' Davis poured another shot of the amber liquid into his glass.

Cole looked across the sawdust to the card-table.

'I'm the only one who can swear in a posse, Pate. Only the sheriff can do that. If'n them boys ride with ya and ya find old Trask and hang him, you'll all be murderers. The law will then either hang ya or send ya all to jail.'

The five men who were willingly sipping Davis's whiskey all made a disturbed noise at exactly the same time. The sheriff's words were not what any of them had expected to hear.

'Hush up, boys,' Davis ordered as he returned his boot to the floor and sat upright. He pointed a finger in the direction of the lawman. 'Ya trying to scare my boys, Cole?'

The sheriff smirked.

'Nope. Just telling it as it is, Pate. The law's the law. I can't change that.'

'But ya can bend the law, Cole.

Right?' Pate Davis stared across the distance between them like a buzzard studying a fresh carcass. 'I've done know a heap of lawmen in my time and most were trash. But not you. You know a little more than most. That's why me and Ben let ya live. The law can be bent if'n a man wants it bad enough.'

The sheriff nodded.

'It can be bent a little, I guess.'

'Then I reckon that you ought to make us all ya deputies. Right?' Davis glared at Cole. 'Then we can hunt down the killin' varmint and make him pay.'

Sheriff Cole cleared his throat silently and ran his finger around in the stale beer on top of the bar. He looked up at the nervous bartender before licking his dried lips and looking back at the outlaw.

'I ought to do just that. I would if I figured it would help me live a little longer, Pate. Trouble is, I just don't cotton to being used by a man with revenge burning into his soul. Nope, I reckon that I ain't gonna swear in no deputies.'

Davis rested the whiskey-glass on the table and rose. The five men around him backed away in every direction. Even plied with a gut full of hard liquor, they all knew how to avoid being caught in a potential deadly crossfire.

'Say that again, you old fool.'

Barney Cole pushed himself away from the bar and turned to face the outlaw. It was the bravest thing he had done in more than forty years.

'I said that I ain't fixing to swear in no posse, Pate. Not now or at any time in the near future.'

Davis blinked hard and a twisted grin etched his unshaven features.

'Ya tired of livin', old-timer?'

Cole shrugged his shoulders.

'Nope. But at my age there ain't a lot left I can still do that I used to be able to do. Reckon that life ain't so valuable to me as it is to a younger man. Ya mad, Pate. Mad with grief and mad to kill anyone that gets in ya way. Denver Ben knew that and he kept ya on a short rein. But now without him, ya just boilin' over. Admit it, son. You don't give a tinker's cuss about ya brother. All ya wanna do is kill. Me or Trask or both. Admit it, Pate!'

Davis hardly knew what to do or say as the harsh but true words sank into his brain. He stepped away from the table and flexed his fingers above the wooden grips of the well-used Remingtons.

'Ya say that I'm mad but how loco are you, Cole? To get me angry is just plain stupid. I've killed men for a darn sight less than that. Ya must have a death wish.'

Barney Cole nodded as he squared up to the approaching outlaw.

'Am I loco, Pate? Or just sick of seeing ya throw ya weight around in my town? Which is it? I sure ain't got it figured. All I know for sure is that I'm the law here. Ain't done my job for the longest while, but maybe I ought to start right about now. What ya think?'

'I think ya gonna die, Sheriff!' Davis was less than ten feet away from the lawman and getting closer with every second that passed.

The lawman inhaled and screamed.

'Since I told ya about Denver Ben, ya ain't even bothered to see him. Ya ain't even enquired where his body is. All ya have had thoughts about is getting even with Trask.'

Pate Davis stopped in his tracks. His face suddenly altered as he realized Cole was right.

'You're an old fool but I reckon ya right. I ought to be paying my last respects to Ben. Damn it all! I never even thought about that. Where'd they take his body, Cole?'

The lawman felt his heart start to beat again inside his chest. Somehow he had survived but it was not over yet and he knew it.

'He's resting in Mo Hardin's back room. That was the only place with a cold slab,' Cole replied. 'We ain't got no funeral parlour here in Hickory.'

'Mo Hardin's place?' Davis looked confused.

'The butcher shop,' the sheriff added.

'The butcher shop? They took Denver Ben to a stinkin' butcher shop?' Davis seemed disturbed by the thought and rubbed his face with both hands. 'That ain't no nice place for a gent like him to be taken. Ain't ya got no respect?'

Cole began to feel that he had at last earned the right to wear the star that was pinned on his vest.

'Murphy at the livery is making a coffin. We thought that a cold marble slab would keep Ben fresh until the funeral. There was nothin' else we could do, Pate.'

Davis nodded and wandered aimlessly around the saloon muttering to himself. He looked at the faces of the men he had forced to agree to following him after Trask as if they were not there. He then circled the card-table, lifted the bottle up and took a long swallow from its neck before

59

throwing it at a wall.

The glass shattered into countless slivers. The fiery liquid ran down the saloon wall. It would be just another stain to join so many others.

'Yeah, that sounds OK. Makes sense. Okay. Take me to Denver Ben, Cole,' Davis shouted.

'When?'

'Now!'

'C'mon, Pate. I'll take ya to see ya brother.' Barney Cole felt as if every muscle in his body were crumbling as he led the outlaw out of the saloon into the dimly lit main street. He had never been so frightened in all his long days.

Davis placed a hand out and caught one of the swing-doors.

'Are you shaking, Cole?'

The sheriff glanced over his shoulder before leading the way along the wide boardwalk toward Hardin's butcher shop. For the first time in all the years that he had worn the sheriff's star in the remote settlement, Cole knew that he would have to do something decisive.

He had to outwit the deadly outlaw who, he knew, could kill faster than most folks could blink. There was a way to get the better of the fiery Pate Davis that did not sit well with the veteran lawman.

Cole knew that he had to somehow convince Davis that he was as vile and corrupt as the outlaw was himself.

'I'm cold, Pate. Just cold.'

'Reckon ya gettin' old.' Davis spat as he trailed the nervous sheriff.

'I ain't gettin' old, Pate. I am old,' Cole corrected.

The sound of Davis's spurs echoed around the wooden storefronts as the two men approached the butcher's store.

To Cole the spurs reminded him of his younger days when he had lived in grander surroundings. The spurs sounded like the bells that hung around the necks of undertakers' well-matched teams back East. He could see the plumed black horses that pulled highly decorated hearses through the streets towards their ultimate destination. He opened the unlocked side door and entered the cool interior. Sides of beef hung all around them.

The sheriff struck a match, touched the wick of a candle and led the way towards the cold-room door.

'C'mon, Pate. He's in here.'

6

For the first time since learning of his brother's fate, Pate Davis suddenly realized what death meant when it came close enough to touch kinfolk. Even on the marble slab, the ashen face of Denver Ben still had the same startled expression on it as it had when Trask's deadly bullets had passed through his silk vest into his heart. Pate Davis walked around the slab in the centre of the butcher's cold-room, silently trying to accept the fact that his brother would never again move or lead them into another of his devious money-making schemes.

'He looks kinda odd,' Davis said at last. 'Not dead at all but sorta like he's asleep or somethin', Cole.'

'Yep. Dead folks gotta habit of looking like that, Pate,' Cole agreed as he pulled his pipe from his pants' pocket and checked its stem.

'He don't look dead though. You looks worse than Ben does, old-timer,' Davis protested. He then rested his hands next to the shoulders of his dead brother and studied Denver Ben's face. 'I don't get it. Nobody was faster with his guns than Ben. Exceptin' me, that is.'

'He's dead OK, Pate,' the lawman said, as his remaining teeth firmly gripped the stem of his pipe. 'The reason he don't look it is because he never expected Trask to be so darn fast. Denver Ben didn't think that Trask could beat him to the draw. Ben looks like he still don't believe it.'

Pate Davis clenched both his fists.

'Ya all said that Trask was a real old guy. How could anyone like that beat the likes of Ben?'

Cole inhaled and tasted the flavour of ten years of tobacco juice fill his mouth. He removed the pipe and spat at the floor before moving to Davis's side.

'I know it sounds loco, but Trask just

stood there. I don't think he even looked at ya brother. Ben went for his guns. The old man slapped leather. The next thing we all knew was that the guns were in Trask's hands. They spewed lead and Denver Ben was blown off his feet. I never seen nothing like it.'

Pate turned away from the lifeless body.

'What happened? How come there was a showdown in the first place?'

'Trask rode into town and went into the saloon,' the sheriff started. 'He saw Ben roughing up someone and seemed to know that Ben was wanted. He called him out. That was that.'

'I've gotta get this Trask varmint, Cole. Ya gotta help me get the old fool.' Pate snorted. 'I've gotta kill him for old Ben's sake. An eye for an eye.'

Sheriff Cole walked out of the store-room and tried to get the smell of meat out of his nostrils. He struck a match and dragged its flame into the pipe-bowl. He puffed until his head was surrounded by aromatic blue smoke. The lawman heard the steps of the outlaw trail him out into the street. He rested his back against a wooden upright.

He had an idea.

'But you're a wanted outlaw with a bounty on ya head. I can't go makin' you a deputy to hunt down Trask. It ain't legal.'

'There ain't no law in these parts.' Pate Davis snorted even harder. 'Only you. I could do anything I wanted if'n you pinned a star on me and you know it. Who'd know that me and the boys weren't real deputies? Only you.'

Cole had known that the Davis brothers were both wanted dead or alive the moment they rode into Hickory Creek. Yet he had chosen to bury his head to the fact and ignore them. Even when they had started to get rough with the residents of the small remote settlement and killed innocent people, he had not stood up to them for fear of his life. It had taken an

66

aging gunfighter named Trask to show him that he had been wrong.

'Do ya truly figure that you'd be able to take Trask?' Cole asked.

'Ya said he was old. I could outdraw him with one eye shut, Sheriff,' Davis said as he stood beside the lawman.

'I also said he was fast. Faster than anyone I ever done seen with a pair of six-shooters, Pate.' Barney Cole continued to puff on the pipe. 'Ya don't wanna end up making the same mistake ya brother made.'

Davis pulled a twisted cigar from his pocket and placed it between his teeth. He leaned over and lit it from the glowing pipe-bowl. He inhaled the strong acrid smoke, then grinned. It was the same devilish grin he had shown to every one of his victims over the years.

'Denver Ben was fast but he also didn't know about Trask. I do know about that old bastard and he ain't gonna get the better of me. He'll die all right. Ya can bet ya bottom dollar on that, Cole. All ya gotta do is supply me with them stars and I'll do the rest.'

'OK,' Cole heard himself say. 'I'll give ya a star. Hell, I'll give ya a box of stars if that's what ya want. You can ride after Trask and kill the critter with the law on ya side. I'll swear that Trask shot Denver Ben in cold blood and you were just tracking down a killer. That suit ya, Pate?'

Pate Davis blew a long line of cigar smoke into the cool night air.

'I told Denver Ben that you was our kinda lawman, Cole. He wanted to kill ya but I said that we ought to give ya a chance to prove yaself.'

'You sure that it was Ben that wanted to kill me, Pate?' the sheriff asked. 'And not you?'

'OK. Maybe it was me that wanted to fill ya with lead,' Davis admitted. 'It don't matter none. You've proved that you're on my side and that counts.'

Barney Cole pushed the glowing tobacco down into the pipe-bowl with his thumb.

'Yep.'

'You go round up them stars and I'll round up my boys. Reckon it'll be dawn before we get ourselves some provisions sorted but that's OK. Trask ain't gonna get far up that trail with the weather closing in on his ancient hide. Soon as it's daylight, I'll lead them boys up into the high country after him. When we catch up with him, it'll be him or me. I reckon ya know who'll win that fight, old-timer.'

Sheriff Barney Cole sucked wryly on his pipe and allowed the smoke to drift from his mouth. He looked through his bushy eyebrows at the outlaw and nodded.

'Yep, I got me a feelin' that I do know who'll win that showdown, Pate.'

7

It was almost eight in the morning before the sun managed to crawl above the mountain peaks that fringed the skyline around the remote Hickory Creek. Sheriff Cole had not slept since he had left the still brooding Pate Davis a handful of hours earlier. All he had done was make one pot of coffee after another in the small office. The elderly lawman knew that he was running the greatest risk of his entire life by trying to trick the bloodthirsty outlaw.

Yet Cole was tired of hiding behind his star. He had allowed his age to become an excuse for not standing up to the Davis brothers when they had first arrived. He had seen men beaten and killed by the deadly duo.

Now it was time to act.

And he had acted like a seasoned professional thespian from the stages back East. No actor could have so thoroughly convinced Pate Davis that he was on his side, the way that Barney Cole had done.

It had taken every ounce of his courage to stand before the lethal outlaw and lie through his teeth that he was willing to help him capture and kill Trask.

The sound of the horses heading along the street filled the small sheriff's office and drew his attention from his umpteenth cup of coffee.

Cole walked out on to the boardwalk and forced a mock smile up at the lead rider. Davis returned the smile with one of his own. Yet there was a difference in the smiles. One was merely a fake whilst the other was tinted by evil.

'Got them stars ya promised, Cole?' Davis asked. He steadied his mount beside the hitching rail and leaned on the saddle horn. 'I got me my posse together and they're eager to get on the trail.'

'I got ya stars, Pate.' Cole fished in

his deep pants'-pocket and offered the six gleaming deputy stars to the outlaw. His eyes studied the faces of the five riders. None looked like he was a willing volunteer.

Davis snatched the deputy stars and laughed.

'I knew ya was OK, Cole. Ya never did give me and Denver Ben any trouble in all the time we was here.'

'Why should I have bothered, boy?' The sheriff shrugged. 'I get paid the same for turning a blind eye as I do for risking my hide. I knew that you boys were OK. Them stars will cover ya tails whatever ya do to that Trask critter.'

Davis pinned a star to his top coat and then dished out the stars to the five men he had paid to ride with him.

'Darn it. I feel real official, Cole,' Davis announced, rubbing the shining star with his coat-sleeve.

'So ya should, Pate.' The lawman nodded. 'That gives ya the right to do whatever ya likes. Now you're a real posse.'

'Hear that, boys?' Davis chuckled over his shoulder at the grim-faced riders. 'We're real honest-to-goodness deputies. We can do what the heck we likes and there ain't nobody that'll stand in our way.'

Barney Cole stepped forward until his boots were on the edge of the boardwalk. He raised his right hand and cleared his throat.

'Raise ya hands, boys.'

The six horsemen did as instructed.

'I deputize you boys in the name of the law,' Cole said.

'I owe ya, Cole.' Pate Davis dragged his reins up to his chest and laughed.

'No problem, Pate.' The sheriff lowered his hand and watched as the riders dragged the necks of their mounts around and then spurred hard.

He remained on the boardwalk until they were out of sight and headed up to the high country. Only when the sound of their pounding hoofs could no longer be heard, did he turn and start to walk down the street.

Exactly twenty-three steps later, Cole turned a doorknob and entered the telegraph office.

'Howdy, Barney,' the telegraph operator said as he watched the lawman rest a hip on the edge of his desk. 'What can I do for ya?'

Cole gritted his teeth around the well-chewed pipe-stem and inhaled deeply several times. He could feel sweat running down his spine even though it was cold. Sweat that denoted how scared he was of crossing the deadly outlaw Pate Davis.

'Are you OK, Barney?' There was concern in the telegraph operator's voice.

The lawman pushed his hat off his brow and swallowed.

'Yep. I'm just frightened. Ya can send a message for me, Mike. A message that I should have sent weeks back.'

'OK.' The man licked the end of his pencil and rested his hand next to the small notepad. 'Shoot.'

'It's to Colonel John Edison. Fort

Wayne,' Cole started. 'Mark it urgent.'

'This sounds darn important, Sheriff,' said the seated man as he jotted down every word the lawman uttered. 'I never seen you send no wires to the army before. Yep. This sounds darn important to me.'

'It is, Mike. It sure is,' Cole muttered.

8

They had once been part of a great tribe that boasted more than 10,000 souls. They had lived on the western side of the vast plains since time itself had started. They had hunted the game and waited for the passing buffalo which then roamed by the million. Their lives had been hard and yet they had wanted for nothing.

Then everything had changed. For reasons that they could not understand, their entire way of life disappeared. At first it was the fact that fewer and fewer buffalo entered the unmarked boundaries of their land.

Then there were none.

Faced with starvation and forced to travel further from their well-established lands and hunting-grounds than they had ever done before, the tribe had found themselves faced with enemies whom they had never imagined existed.

Both red and white foes soon began to destroy the ancient civilization that had lived peacefully for centuries in total isolation.

Within a mere decade, they had met the same fate that had befallen their cousins on the east coast and almost totally disappeared from the face of the map. Only small, disoriented groups remained: embittered and ruthless souls who roamed aimlessly far from the land which had nurtured them and which others now occupied.

Red Eagle stood on a large rock staring down into what seemed an endless sea of trees. Mist rose up into the air from the treetops as the morning sun spread like a blanket over them. Yet there was little warmth in the golden orb.

There were only thirty-two warriors left from what had once numbered more than the leaves on the proudest of oaks. Red Eagle was their reluctant leader; the one man who had been able to lead his small party away from the relentless bloodbath that their existence had become.

The noble brave knew that if any others of his tribe still lived, it was doubtful that he or any of his warriors would ever encounter them again.

Red Eagle knew that his was a slender leadership: one that he might not be able to retain for much longer. For most of his younger followers had already turned their weaponry on those who lived in these forests.

The silver-haired Indian had seen the last of his people become even more brutal than the distant enemies who had destroyed his tribe.

They had shown no mercy to either white- or red-skinned people since their arrival in the high country.

It sickened Red Eagle and yet he understood the reasons behind the desperate and lethal atrocities. For they had lost everything: their land, their women and their futures.

They were the last of their people.

Vengeance was all they had left.

Red Eagle could still smell the distant campfire somewhere to the north of where he stood. He knew that its aroma would soon entice his warriors to track down whoever had made camp the previous night.

For they were driven by only one basic instinct now.

To kill.

Red Eagle glanced over his shoulder at his braves as they dragged the heavy furs over their scarred torsos. His heart sank for what felt like the millionth time when he saw them smearing war paint over their chiselled features. They had the scent of fresh prey in their nostrils. Only killing would quench the bloody thirst of his men.

Reluctantly, Red Eagle would lead them again.

9

Waldo Zane was a man who was as good as his word. By dawn he had skinned the large black bear and strapped its pelt to the back of his grey. With all the other furs weighing the animal down it was hard to see the horse itself. Then he had extinguished the fire and led his injured companion far from their makeshift campsite.

More asleep than awake, the gunfighter knew little of what was going on. Trask had been mounted for more than an hour before the first birds' chorus started to herald the new day. His torn shirt had been replaced by several animal pelts which the mountain man had crudely sewn together to make a makeshift coat.

Brief glimpses of daylight filtering through the trees began to draw Trask's attention. He started to take interest in the situation he found himself in.

The gunfighter sat astride his stallion with both his hands resting on the saddle horn next to the gun grips which sat proudly in the gunbelt.

Trask yawned and looked around at the unfamiliar terrain they had been travelling through since long before he had truly awoken. Most of the trees were long thin pines growing so close together that they resembled fenceposts.

Bushes fought for what little sunlight managed to penetrate the canopy high above them and filled most of the gaps between the trees. A few larger broad-leafed trees were scattered through the forest, already shedding their foliage in anticipation of the impending winter.

The further they rode, the darker the cold woodlands became. Trask leaned back against his saddle cantle and looked straight upward. Only the briefest of moments allowed any sight of the sun far above the forest. Pitiful shafts of sun-rays vainly cut through the branches trying to find the ground beneath their horses' hoofs.

Mist rolled a few feet above the ground in all directions and floated like phantoms seeking their long-lost graves. There was a blackness beyond the trees as if it were still night less than a score of yards from where they rode.

Trask rubbed the sleep from his eyes.

He could still not see anything clearly except the horseman ahead of him and the rope which joined both mounts together.

Zane had used his lariat to secure the bridle of Trask's stallion to his own heavily laden mount's saddle. Trask trailed the huge rider and wondered how the grey horse ahead of him could carry not only the incredible amount of furs but also the hefty mountain man.

Since they had set out the riders had not been close enough to speak to one another. Waldo Zane led and Trask simply followed.

The older man wondered where they

were headed. For the first half-hour or so they had kept to the trail and ridden up hill but then they had left the trail and started to descend through the trees. Trask tried to work out why Waldo had veered off the trail and headed into virgin forest.

Then he remembered the previous evening around the camp-fire and how the trapper had claimed to have heard Indians somewhere off in the distance. Had Zane actually heard them or was it merely the imagination of a lonely mountain man?

Trask gently tapped his spurs into the flesh of his stallion and let the tall animal know that its master was now in full control of him.

They rode deeper into the uncharted woodlands.

There was barely enough room between the tall straight pines for their horses to navigate, yet Zane pressed on and on. Every now and then the trapper would look over his shoulder as if to make sure that his companion's horse was still secured to the lariat. At last Trask managed to summon the strength to speak.

'I'm still here, big fella.'

'About time you woked up, old-timer.'

'How come we're heading away from the trail?'

'Injuns!' Zane muttered. 'Them Injuns made better time gettin' to our camp than I thought they would. I reckon we only got away with a matter of minutes to spare.'

'They got horses?'

'Yep. Darn sturdy little critters.'

Trask looked around them.

'Are they close?'

'Yep. Darn close.'

'How can you tell?' Trask asked. There was an urgency in his voice. 'I can't see nothing except mist and shadows out there. How can you tell?'

'Gosh darn it. Use ya ears and ya nose, Trask!' Waldo snapped. 'Not ya eyes. Ya eyes ain't no good in this kinda country. Ya gotta listen and sniff.

They're out there and they're gettin' closer.'

Every sound dragged Trask's eyes away from the horseman before him. Trask was nervous and still hurting from the bullet wound he sported in his side. He tried to do as the lead rider had said, but could neither hear or smell anything except their mounts and the furs.

'How many are there, Waldo?'

'Too many.' Zane sighed loudly. 'Way too many.'

The gunfighter flicked the safety loops off his gun hammers and patted the gunbelt with the palm of his right hand. If trouble was brewing, Trask was ready.

Suddenly, without warning, Waldo reined in and dropped heavily off the grey. The big man held the nose of his horse firmly and listened with an intensity that Trask had never seen before in anyone except another gunfighter a few seconds before a showdown.

Trask held his own mount in check until the massive man moved to his side. Their eyes met.

'What's wrong, Waldo?' Trask asked in a hushed tone.

'Ain't sure, Trask,' the trapper admitted. 'I reckon that they're out there. On foot. A hell of a lot of 'em. They've dismounted and spread out as far as I can tell. I don't like it none.'

The gunfighter felt his hands encircle the pair of Colts before him as they had done countless times before.

'The Indians?'

Waldo Zane screwed up his eyes.

'Might be. Could be game. Deers or the like. I ain't too sure. But my money's on the Injuns, old man.'

Trask swallowed hard.

'I can't hear nothing at all except our horses breathing.'

Waldo pushed his mane of unkempt hair away from his eyes and squinted into the darkness beyond the mist.

'I still can't get a fix on anything,' Trask said as his hands slid the magnificent guns from their holsters. 'But if you say that there's something out there, I reckon I ain't loco enough to argue.'

Zane looked at the guns and then up at the face of the older man. He had seen many faces in his time. All sorts of faces but none that seemed as honest as Trask's. The weaponry and the man did not seem to belong together.

'You any good with them guns, old-timer?'

Trask smiled.

'I've been known to hit what I'm aiming at.'

The mountain man swung around on his heels and looked to right and then left.

'Ya must have heard that!'

'Nope.' Trask used his thumbs to haul back the hammers of the weapons in his hands. 'Reckon I ought to dismount? I make a darn easy target up here.'

Waldo shook his head and moved around the tall stallion as if trying to locate the exact origin of the sound he could hear echoing off the trees around them.

'Stay where ya is,' Zane ordered as he reached the other side of Trask's horse's saddle. 'Ya might have to use them darn spurs in a hurry and ya ain't young or fit enough to get back on this tall horse fast enough.'

The veteran gunfighter watched silently as Zane moved back his own horse. The huge hands dragged the buffalo gun from beneath the still-fresh bear skin and the array of other pelts.

Zane swiftly loaded the heavy weapon.

'It's the Injuns all right. Now I'm certain. They must have ridden around us and now the varmints are on foot. They're closin' in for the kill!'

'Waldo! I hear something now. Over yonder,' Trask said as a noise to his left caught his attention. He turned in his saddle and balanced in his stirrups. His guns aimed at the sound which was getting closer.

Zane cocked the large hammer of his rifle and stepped around the head of his grey.

'Steady now, Curly. We got us some unwanted company.'

The grey snorted as if it understood every word that its master said.

Trask felt his heart start to increase its pace inside his chest. He gritted his teeth and watched his newly found saviour raise the buffalo gun up until he was staring down the gleaming barrel.

'Better hold on to ya hoss darn tight, Trask. Reckon this'll spook him a tad,' Waldo said before looping his index finger around its trigger.

Trask pushed the weapon in his left hand back into its holster and then wrapped the reins around his wrist. He dragged the head of his stallion back and waited.

'Here they come,' Waldo Zane growled.

For what felt like a lifetime, they saw nothing as the sound of branches snapping underfoot grew ever louder.

Then both Trask and Zane caught sight of the brightly coloured war paint.

Red Eagle and his warriors ran through the mist screaming at the tops of their voices.

The blood-chilling sound of the Indians' war cries filled the air.

A dozen or more bullets blasted from the barrels of the Indians' rifles as they suddenly emerged from the ghostly mist.

Zane squeezed his trigger.

A thunderclap could not have made more noise. The cloud of smoke trailed the deadly cartridge until the bullet hit one of the charging warriors. There was little left of the Indian after the impact.

Waldo Zane did not wait to see the result of his handiwork. He ripped the end of his lariat from the stallion's bridle, turned and threw himself on to his saddle. He used the barrel of his rifle to whip the grey into action. The animal responded immediately.

'C'mon, Trask!' Waldo yelled over his

shoulder. 'This bunch don't take no prisoners!'

Red-hot tapers of deadly lead tore through the half-light, seeking the two horsemen.

Trask felt his Stetson torn from his head. He could see that every one of the braves was armed with repeating rifles. He sank his spurs into the flesh of his stallion and drove after the fleeing mountain man. Bullets ripped branches off trees as the stallion charged after the tail of the grey.

As Trask spurred his horse on, he fired blindly under his arm at the Indians as rifle bullets continued to cut through the morning air. A thousand angry hornets could never have made more noise. Trask could feel the heat of the deadly lead venom as it sought his life.

The terrified horse crashed through the brush and negotiated a route through the trees.

The two horsemen felt the trail beneath the hoofs of their mounts fall away as they started to descend rapidly. Neither rider had any idea where they were or where they were headed. All they knew for sure was that they had to try and outride the lethal rifle bullets. Chunks of tree-bark were torn to shreds all about them and splintered into a million fragments.

The horses ended up on their knees as the ground levelled out. The riders hauled back on their reins and dragged their mounts back up on to their feet. They drove on again. Trask managed to draw level when both horses were faced with another steep muddy slope.

'What kinda Indians were they, Waldo?' the gufighter shouted across at his companion.

'Damn angry ones, old-timer!' Zane shouted back. 'Just keep ridin' hard!'

Both horses charged down the slippery slope and then drove on through the another stand of towering trees. The grey started to pull away from the stallion once more.

'But how come we gotta keep riding

hard, Waldo?' Trask asked and steered his horse after the grey and whipped its shoulders with his reins. 'We're out of range now!'

'Listen, ya old fool,' Zane shouted back at Trask. 'They've mounted up again. They're still after our tails!'

Trask turned his head as both his hands urged the horse to find even greater speed. At first he thought it was thunder. Then he realized that it was the rumbling sound of more than thirty horses forging their way through the dense forest after them.

He spurred hard.

10

Pate Davis was more than a hundred yards ahead of the men he had paid to accompany him into the forested high country when he heard the ominous sounds of rifle- and gunfire drifting through the tall pines. He leaned back against his saddle cantle and hauled on his reins until his horse stopped abruptly.

Then, as quickly as it seemed to have started, the noise ceased. Davis balanced, holding his horse's head in check as his men caught up to him.

The five riders slowed to a halt and waited as the troubled outlaw silently stood in his stirrups and surveyed the eerie forest landscape. Davis pulled at his reins and the horse slowly turned full circle on the trail. He was no tracker but even he could see the hoof-tracks left by Trask's stallion on the soft ground that led up through the dark trees.

One of the riders, called Strother Jackson, eased his mount alongside the infamous outlaw's lathered-up horse.

'What's wrong, Pate? The old-timer's hoof-tracks are plain as plain can be. A blind man could follow them. How come ya damn well stopped?'

Pate Davis steadied his skittish mount.

'Ain't the tracks that's troublin' me, Stroth. I'm damn sure I heard me some gunplay way over that ridge.'

'When?' Jackson asked.

'When we was ridin' up here.'

Another of the riders, called Luke Parsons, teased his gelding forward. He had almost sobered up during the long ride to this cold, unforgiving place.

'I thought that was thunder, Pate. Sounded like thunder to me.'

'Weren't no thunder, Luke!' Davis snorted as he spun the horse around and returned his attention to where the trail went over the ridge ahead of them. 'That was shootin'. Somebody ahead of us has been shootin'. But who? Where? And why?'

'Must be Trask again!' Jackson suggested. 'The old coot is probably gun-happy. Ya know the sort? They just gotta shoot at things. Ya see it every Saturday night. Some folks even take pot shots at the moon.'

Pate Davis's eyes narrowed as he leaned on his saddle horn and brooded. He was confused. As far as he knew there was only one rider on this remote unforgiving mountainside and that was Trask. The shots had proved him wrong.

'I heard me too many shots for it to be just one loco old-timer like Trask. Nope, I heard me a lotta shots.'

The faces of Davis's companions were blank. None had heard what their paymaster had heard above the sound of their galloping horses. Yet they had been a long way behind Davis.

Jackson rubbed the deputy's star on

his chest thoughtfully and gave a half-smile.

'Maybe its a bunch of outlaws, Pate. We could arrest the varmints and get the reward money.'

Davis glanced at the smiling horseman. His face was deadly serious.

'Not a bad idea, Stroth. But I got me a bad feelin' in my guts about this. I figure that Trask has ridden into trouble of a very different sort.'

'What kinda trouble?' another of the men asked.

'I ain't sure,' Pate Davis admitted, his teeth biting his lower lip. 'If'n there was outlaw gangs up here in the high country, I'm sure me and Denver Ben would have heard about them. What other sort of folks would shoot at Trask? I thought this forest was deserted.'

'I still reckon ya heard thunder, Pate,' Parsons chipped in again.

Davis straightened up in his saddle and gathered his loose reins together. He pulled a twisted cigar remnant from his shirt pocket and placed it between his teeth. He chewed the tobacco and fumbled for a match. He found one, struck it across his saddle horn and cupped the flame.

'There ain't no Injuns up in these trees, are there?' Davis asked as smoke billowed from his mouth.

Jackson's jaw dropped.

'Hell! I reckon there might be, Pate. Come to think about it, I did hear some tales . . . '

Davis sucked in a lungful of smoke. 'Ya got any other secrets ya might like to tell us about, Stroth?'

The other four horsemen started to get nervous. Davis pulled the cigar from his mouth and pointed its smoking tip at them. His eyes burned like pokers.

'Don't none of you boys start frettin' about no Injuns. 'Coz if ya try and turn tail on me, I'll kill ya! OK?'

The men nodded silently. They knew that Pate meant every single word that had come from his mouth. He was far more dangerous than anything they might find on their journey through the forested mountains.

Then the sound of even more deafening shots echoed out all around them. Davis pushed the cigar back into his teeth and grabbed his reins in both hands.

'Hear that? C'mon! Let's go kill us some vermin, boys!'

The riders spurred. The six horses galloped up the steep trail between the trees and headed straight towards the sound of rifles and six-shooters.

11

The stench of gunsmoke filled the damp forest interior. Red Eagle waved his rifle around in a circle above his head and watched as his braves fanned out to both sides of him and drove their painted ponies down through the tree-covered slopes. They had closed the gap between themselves and the two fleeing riders they had pursued until they were only a matter of fifty yards apart.

The skilled native horsemen could keep their ponies moving at full speed through the hostile terrain whilst they used their hands to repeatedly fire their rifles.

Deafening explosions tortured the eardrums of the pair of riders. Deadly lead rained down at them from both sides as well as from behind. Only the multitude of trees through which they continued to force their mounts shielded them from the bullets finding their targets.

Hot, smouldering sawdust filled the eyes of the mounts as well as those of their masters, yet they drove on and on. There was no time to hesitate. To pause for even the briefest of moments would mean almost certain death.

And both Waldo Zane and Trask knew it.

The mountain man continued to thrash the grey beneath him with the barrel of his buffalo gun but he knew that the exhausted horse was no match for the agile Indian mounts.

He dragged his reins from one side to another and forced the horse to zigzag between the trees. The power of the Indians' bullets ripped into the furs worn by the lead rider yet Zane continued on. Trask used the long lengths of his reins to whip the shoulders of his stallion and chased the mountain man. With every long stride of the frightened animal beneath his saddle, the gunfighter wondered if any of the shots had actually hit Zane.

Then Trask caught a brief glimpse of water to his left and pulled the stallion around.

'Waldo! This way!'

Zane twisted the neck of the grey and crashed through a wall of brush. Thorns tore at the flesh of the small horse as the rider chased after the gunfighter.

'What ya seen?' he yelled out blindly as his long buffalo gun urged the mount on.

'Water!' Trask replied as his mount leapt out into mid-air.

'Hope it ain't a waterfall, old-timer!' Waldo Zane growled as his grey jumped after the stallion.

Trask did not reply. It was all he could do to remain in his saddle. Water sparkled beneath him as a few rays of sun managed to break through the tree canopies. He felt his horse falling into a place he suddenly realized might be the end of him.

A thousand thoughts raced through his mind.

What if the water was shallow? That would mean almost certain death or worse!

Then he felt the impact as water enveloped them. His horse sank into the deep river and he was dragged down with it. The water moved him violently to the side as the grey horse also entered the river with its heavy load.

The current was swift and dragged both horses and their masters beneath its ice-cold surface. They were washed downriver for what felt like miles.

Trask and Zane fought for their lives to find a precious gasp of air to fill their lungs.

12

There were a half-dozen well-constructed log cabins surrounding the trading post at Cooper's Point. Each was made of long straight pines from the surrounding forest that covered the mountainous peaks which rolled on for as far as the eye could see. A mere two miles along the Bighorn River from the massive army outpost of Fort Wayne, Cooper's Point still drew the mysterious creatures known as mountain men to trade their furs as it had done for nearly thirty years.

It was as if few if any females ever ventured into the harsh and dangerous land around the trading post. Those who did were as big as the men they accompanied and twice as ornery. They seldom accompanied their men to the trading post.

Joshua Cooper was like the rest of his

rare breed. He was big. Not just tall, but of gigantic proportions. And, like the other mountain men, probably doomed to live less than three score years. For unlike the ageless trees which dominated the landscape, the big men burned themselves out far faster than their less sturdy cousins.

Joshua Cooper ruled Cooper's Point as his late father had done before him. He alone traded the furs on the Western Woodland with the eager buyers from back East. Unlike the agents, he was known for always giving the best price for quality goods.

Things had been peaceful along the narrow valley beside the fast-flowing river for over a decade. Even Indians used the remote trading post to trade.

Yet something was gnawing at his craw.

Cooper had been uncharacteristically restless for the previous month. He sensed that something was wrong up in the green ocean of trees that surrounded the tiny settlement of cabins.

Half a dozen of the trappers that regularly traded their furs with him had failed to show up. Cooper knew that this was highly unusual. Mountain men seemed to have a fantastic sense of time and had the ability to arrive at his trading post usually within a day of an agreed date. How they managed this feat was something which he had never been able to fathom, but it was a fact. The bearded men kept better time than most clocks or calendars.

Cooper knew that the forests were anything but hospitable, yet most of the seasoned trappers had managed to keep their agreed appointments, until now. Every season always claimed at least one of the trappers through either accident or age, but for so many suddenly to fail to appear was alarming.

Joshua Cooper chewed on a lump of tobacco and stared from his porch at the mist-covered trees a few miles across the river. So many trees that it was impossible even to imagine their true numbers.

The huge man spat for the ump-teenth time at the ground. His aim was so accurate that each lump of black goo landed within a few inches of the previous one.

As Cooper chewed, he was thought-ful.

Where were the trappers? It was a question that had begun to haunt the massive man. Cooper stroked the tobacco-stained beard which reached and covered his broad belt. Most of the cabins around him were unoccupied and that was something he had never experienced before. Usually there were always enough weary mountain men to fill the log cabins in the past. He had seen times when he had been forced to make three of the massive men share a cabin.

Not now.

Now Cooper's Point was virtually deserted. With winter only a handful weeks away Joshua Cooper knew that the mountain men should be buying provisions to tide them over the most severe months.

The big man gritted his stained teeth.

The sun had cleared the highest of the mountains less than an hour earlier and yet there was little or no heat in its bright rays. Cooper continued to chew and study the distant tree-line across the Bighorn River.

If anyone rode out on to flat grassland from the forests, he would be the first to see them. The smoke from the blackened chimney on his roof had guided many a lost soul to his door over the lifetime he had spent at the trading post.

It was a frustrated Cooper who eventually turned and entered his large building. His eyes darted around the well-stocked shelves filled with canned goods and fancy luxuries as well as an abundance of hard liquor and ammunition for every known weapon. An assortment of rifles and handguns also hung on nails all around the walls of the trading post. A glass cabinet filled with knives of a score of differing designs gleamed as the sunlight traced across the heart of the cluttered building.

Of all his wares, whiskey, whatever its quality, went down well in these remote parts. Cooper knew that men usually headed straight for the bottles of spirit before anything else. Then his eyes drifted to the dwindling stack of furs.

He opened the cast-iron top of his stove and dropped another two logs into it. As red sparks floated up, he returned the lid and then sat down on a sturdy chair next to it. He continued to look out of the wide-open doorway at the dark green forest beyond the wide river.

Then Cooper saw something.

He rose and strode powerfully across the dirt floor and back out on to the porch. His eyes narrowed and homed in on the two riders who were approaching from the south.

Joshua Cooper instantly recognized the larger rider atop the shaggy-haired grey horse, but could not make out Waldo Zane's companion.

He spat again and walked out into the bright sunlight. He rested his large knuckles on his broad hips and nodded as the pair of horses negotiated the river toward him.

Then Cooper's smile evaporated.

Something was very wrong.

13

Fort Wayne had weathered many storms during its brief but colourful history. Built as a constant reminder to the Shoshoni, Arapaho and Cheyenne along the Bighorn River that the US Army had total control of the long winding valley between the vast tree-covered peaks known as the Western Woodlands at the foot of the Rocky Mountains, it had served its purpose well.

Few of the northern tribes had ever dared to challenge the large well-fortified structure, having witnessed at first hand the sheer fire-power of its 700 soldiers.

Yet there was trouble brewing and Fort Wayne's commanding officer, Colonel John Edison knew it. Every sinew of his six-foot-tall frame told him so. Twinges from old wounds told him that danger was looming over the fortress like buzzards floating on high thermals. Battle-seasoned soldiers of Edison's kind knew that they had to listen to their gut instincts if they were to survive.

In all his fifty-nine years, he had learned never to ignore those instincts. They were the one thing that had allowed him to reach an age when most of his contemporaries were either retired, crippled or just plain dead and buried.

He studied the short telegraph message from Sheriff Barney Cole at his desk and then looked up. The noonday sun that illuminated his large office disguised the fact that there was no heat left in its vibrant rays.

Fall had come earlier this year and that meant trouble for the cavalry officer. For Edison had to ensure not only peace in this hostile land, but also keep his 700 men well fed throughout the long winter months when Fort Wayne was virtually cut off from the rest of civilization.

Remote military outposts were always difficult to run and Fort Wayne had tested the veteran cavalry officer more times than he cared to recall.

'Is the time on this message correct, Captain?' Edison asked the officer who had brought the message to him only minutes earlier.

Captain George O'Hara shrugged.

'I can't say for certain, sir.'

Edison rose and waved the small telegraph message at the nervous officer.

'I only ask, because if the time on this wire is right, somebody managed to sit on the damn thing for more than twelve damn hours!'

'Twelve hours?' O'Hara gulped.

'Yes, Captain. Twelve hours!' The colonel paced around the office, then came to a stop by the window. He looked out at the large parade ground and the scores of buildings which stretched off in all directions bathed in sunlight. 'This message says URGENT on it. I just can't understand why that part of it failed to alert anyone that maybe it ought to be brought to me straight away. Can you?'

'No, sir.'

Edison exhaled loudly. He rested a hip on the window-sill and glared at the pencilled words again.

'Barney Cole has never been a man to go off half-cocked. If he says a message is urgent, it is.'

'I'll ask the men in the telegraph office if they can explain the delay, sir,' the captain stammered.

Edison shook his head.

'Forget it. It's a damn long ride over them mountains from Hickory Creek. The main point is that a certain Mr Pate Davis has a deputy star and is hunting the man called Trask. This man killed Denver Ben Davis, Pate Davis's brother, in a fair fight. But Pate Davis wants to get even with Trask. He has five men with him.'

O'Hara tilted his head.

'I don't understand, sir,' he admitted.

'Pate and Denver Ben are wanted in five States and territories, O'Hara,' Edison said bluntly. 'Dead or alive. This Trask is a gunfighter. I've heard a lot about him over the years. A strange loner who risks his life to help people.'

The look of confusion on the captain's face was genuine. He simply could not understand anything that was not in his West Point handbook.

'With respect, sir, why is Pate Davis a deputy if he's also a wanted outlaw?'

'He isn't a real deputy, you young fool! He forced Sheriff Cole to give him and his riders deputys' stars so that they could hunt down Trask. Now do you understand?'

George O'Hara raised his eyebrows.

'I . . . I'm not sure.'

Colonel Edison grabbed his hat and placed it on his head of white hair, pulled open the door of his office and marched out on to the parade ground. He could hear the feet of the captain a few paces behind him, attempting to keep up. Edison increased his pace until he could hear the younger officer panting like a hound-dog.

'Cole said that Davis and his men are headed up into the forests above Hickory Creek. That trail goes straight to Cooper's Point.'

'Where?' O'Hara gasped.

Edison stopped abruptly and turned to see the captain forced to halt. He pointed a finger at the young tanned face.

'How did you end up here, son? And why? Did I do something to upset the brassnecks back East? Did they send you here to torment me?'

'I don't understand, sir.'

'Cooper's Point is a few miles up river from here. The trading post. Remember the damn trading post we rode to a few months back?'

'I think I do, sir.' The captain nodded.

Edison shook his head again.

'Do you recall my talking with the owner of the trading post, Captain? Please try and remember.'

'Yes, sir!' O'Hara said loudly. 'I do recall you talking to the big man with the dirty beard.'

'Good! That was Josh Cooper.'

'Who?'

'Think about it. Josh Cooper. Cooper's Point! Get the connection here, son?'

O'Hara bit his lip. 'I think so.'

The colonel tried not to shout.

'Cooper told me that some of the mountain men that he does business with had disappeared. He was concerned that they had been killed up in the high country.'

The captain shrugged again.

'He did?'

Edison rested a gloved hand on the young officer's shoulder and tried to keep his voice from bursting the man's eardrums.

'Go to Sergeant Brewster. Tell him I want fifty men ready to ride in exactly one hour from now. I shall lead them to Cooper's Point.'

'But why are you going there, sir?'

Edison squeezed the captain's shoulder until he saw the pain etched on O'Hara's face.

'To try and capture Pate Davis, boy. Because Trask took the trail out of Hickory Creek and that leads to only one place and that happens to be the trading post.'

'Oh.'

The colonel released his grip and watched as the man headed towards the sergeants' mess.

'Tell Brewster to have your horse saddled too, O'Hara.'

'My horse?'

'Of course. You don't think I would ride out to try and capture a deadly outlaw without you at my side, do you?' John Edison lowered his head so that the brim of his hat hid his wry smile from the inexperienced officer.

Captain O'Hara continued on towards the noisy sergeants' mess without uttering another word.

14

Colonel John Edison led his fifty troopers and the reluctant captain as he had always done, from the front. In his youth he had been known as the finest horseman who had ever set foot inside West Point and swiftly became the perfect cavalry officer. He had lost none of his instinctive skill. The powerful charger beneath him would have defeated most riders and yet Edison had the animal totally under his control.

Every one of the enlisted cavalrymen who trailed him knew he was in safe hands. A chest full of battle ribbons told all onlookers that this was no ordinary officer. Edison was cut from a very different cloth from most of his sort who commanded remote cavalry outposts. Unlike his contemporaries Colonel Edison was not at Fort Wayne as a punishment for earlier misdeeds, he was there because the sheer size and military importance of Fort Wayne demanded someone of exceptional quality to command it successfully.

He had done this long before his hair had gone grey.

The troop cut down through the long, sweet grass which surrounded the outpost and went on towards the wide river. Edison had never been a man to send men into a situation that he had doubts about. The telegraph message inside his buttoned-down tunic-pocket troubled him.

Although Sheriff Barney Cole had gone into a lot of detail concerning Pate Davis, the Hickory Creek lawman had not explained everything and the cavalry officer knew it.

Yet it was not that which burned at his innards. It was the fact that for too long, mountain men and even the peaceful natives who lived in the vast uncharted forests had been falling prey to an unseen enemy.

Who was killing people in and around Fort Wayne for no understandable reason?

John Edison wanted answers.

The wire from Sheriff Cole had just been an excuse for Edison to get out of the fortress and investigate in and around Cooper's Point. If there were answers to be found concerning the mysterious disappearances and murders, the experienced officer knew that it was likely that he would find them there.

Tales of a strange band of Indians had grown like a cancer in the isolated fort. Even the supply-wagon train drivers and crew seemed filled with the gossip about them. Edison wondered how much truth there could be in such stories. Someone was killing innocent people and they were using repeating rifles. Whether white- or red-skinned, they had to be stopped.

The colonel had taken it upon himself to do his utmost to stop them, whatever the cost to himself might be.

For he was the protector of this remote region and took his responsibility seriously.

The charger pulled hard as its nostrils filled with the fresh scent of fast-flowing water. Edison allowed the animal its head and left the remainder of his troop far behind him as he drove down towards the Bighorn.

The powerful steed had filled its belly with water long before Captain O'Hara and Sergeant Brewster had led the rest of the cavalrymen to his side.

On the long approach, Brewster had watched his colonel standing holding his reins next to the river. Even in the autumn of his days, the sergeant knew that Edison was still head and shoulders above any other man in the cavalry when it came to knowing every aspect of his job.

Brewster dismounted and tossed his reins to one of the troopers. He walked to the side of the thoughtful colonel and cleared his throat.

'Permission to water the horses, sir?'

Edison touched the brim of his hat. 'Granted.'

Sergeant Brewster turned and shouted at the horsemen.

'Water ya nags and fill ya canteens! We got us a long ride ahead of us.'

Colonel Edison crouched down and stared at the crystal-clear water, which had flowed relentlessly since time itself had begun, and sighed heavily. He looked at the reflections of his favourite enlisted man and then at his own. They had been together through countless campaigns and knew that even the most routine of rides could turn into a bloodbath.

'I think we are starting to look our age, Brewster.'

'Well I sure looks a mite weathered, sir,' the burly sergeant agreed. 'But you looks no older than the day we first met. You still have that spring in your step.'

Edison rose up and gave a hearty belly-laugh.

'Ha! Still the old flatterer, Brewster.'

'It's true.'

The distinguished officer turned away from the rest of his men and leaned closer to the faithful sergeant, a man whom he trusted above all others, and winked.

'The whiskey-bottle is in my saddle-bag. Take a sly snort but don't let anyone see you do it. Not even me. Understood?'

Brewster beamed.

'I knew you was a true gentleman the first time I saved your life, sir.'

'You'll never realize how well that unselfish deed has served you over the years.' Edison nodded and looked upriver. The afternoon sun was getting lower.

'I estimate that we have three hours before sunset.'

The sergeant returned the whiskey-bottle slyly to the saddle-bag and wiped his mouth on his sleeve.

'Plenty of time for us to get to Cooper's Point, sir.'

Thoughtfully Edison toyed with the

reins in his gloved hands. He said nothing as the enlisted man moved around him. Their eyes met.

'Unless you got a mind to go someplace else first,' Brewster whispered.

The colonel knew that after so many years together in a half-dozen different military outposts, Brewster could almost read his mind.

'What would you say if I suggested that we take a slight diversion up into the high country, Brewster?'

'You're thinkin' of them stories about a band of rogue Injuns who are killin' folks around here, ain't ya?'

'Indeed.'

Brewster rubbed his face with his hands as if attempting to clear his thoughts. He inhaled deeply and then looked hard at the man beside him.

'Could be a mite dangerous,' he commented. 'We'll lose the light darn soon and most of these boys are still wet behind the ears and not likely to handle a fight well. That is if we run up against any hostiles, sir. That woodland ain't no place to go ridin' around in with a bunch of children.'

Edison gave a muted laugh. He tugged at the head of his charger and raised it up from the water. He then moved along the animal, stepped into his stirrup and hauled himself up on to the saddle. He looked at the men and his inexperienced captain before returning his attention to the concerned unshaven features next to him.

'As usual you are correct, Brewster. We shall press on to Cooper's Point. Whatever is up in those trees can wait for the moment.'

Brewster gave a wide smile.

'No wonder you have lived so long, Colonel. A military brain that's sharper than a straight razor. Yep, there ain't a smarter officer in the cavalry. Wisdom like yours is a darn rare thing in military officers.'

'I'd quit whilst you're ahead. I'll let you have another ration of red-eye when we reach the trading post at

Cooper's Point, Sergeant Brewster.' Edison turned his mount and faced the men who had total faith in his judgement.

'Get back on your nags, little boys!' Brewster bawled at the troopers. 'The colonel wants to take you all on a lovely little ride.'

John Edison looked down at the smiling Brewster.

'Make that double rations, Sergeant. Flattery that rich deserves reward.'

* * *

Joshua Cooper had known that something was wrong as soon as he set eyes upon the two riders. Both men were bedraggled and seemed barely capable of remaining in their saddles on the slow approach to the trading post.

Men like Waldo Zane seldom displayed their injuries in public and yet even the huge mountain man could not hide the fact that he was hurt bad.

Real bad.

Trask was soaked to the skin like his companion. A mixture of river-water and blood covered him and his mount from head to foot. His white hair was almost crimson from the countless small gashes which covered him: injuries that he had suffered as he had clung desperately to his horse in the savage river-current.

Trask silently trailed the small grey atop his stallion as if he were in a trance, unable to believe what had happened to them both since they had first encountered one another the previous evening. He still could not believe that he and the trapper had survived.

Joshua Cooper had never witnessed two men so obviously injured before and still capable of riding. Usually when anyone looked like them, they were long dead.

'You OK, Waldo?' Cooper shouted as he ran to the shaggy grey's head and grabbed at its bridle. The exhausted animal looked nearly pink with the volume of blood that had soaked its shaggy long hair.

Zane pushed the mane of hair off his face and looked down at the concerned trader.

'Do I *look* OK, Josh? Does either of us look OK? What kinda question is that? We just had the fight of our lives with a bunch of real mean Injuns and then this old fool led us off a cliff and into a damn river. How we or the darn horses didn't drown, I'll never know!'

'Sorry.' Cooper gulped. 'You both looks bad. Darn bad and no mistake.'

Waldo grunted and looked back at Trask.

'Hey, Trask. This is Josh Cooper. He ain't too bright but he's a darn good checker-player. Not that we needs a darn good checker-player. We needs a doctor or a medicine-man.'

'Trask?' Cooper repeated the name. 'I heard that name before someplace.'

'Names are like weeds, Josh,' Zane said as he relaxed in his saddle and allowed Cooper to lead his horse to the hitching rail outside the trading post. 'Names spread out if ya ain't careful. Soon every worthless critter that ever drew a breath knows it. Yep, names are like weeds.'

Cooper looked back at Trask.

'You any idea what Waldo's rantin' about?'

'Nope.'

'You ain't the gunfighter, are you?'

Trask nodded.

'Yep. I'm him.'

'I heard about you. Reckoned it was all a lot of moonshine but there you are. Reckon ya must be real enough.' The trading post owner seemed excited. 'We ain't never had us a gunfighter in these parts before. Even one that looks as beatup and old as you does.'

'Sorry if I don't take any bows, Josh,' Trask said. 'I just feel a tad tuckered out at the moment.'

'You're always tuckered out, Trask!' Waldo grunted. 'Ain't never met a more tuckered-out varmint in all my days. I seen dead folks with more vinegar than you got.'

Cooper stopped walking. He looped the reins of the grey around the hitching rail and tied a secure knot. His eyes then studied the rider on the tall stallion more closely.

'I'd figured that gunfighters would be a lot younger than you are, Trask,' he commented.

Trask drew his reins back and stopped his horse. He remained in his saddle, sucking in the crisp air.

'Reckon I must be a pretty good gunfighter to have lived this long, Josh!'

Zane groaned as he carefully dismounted.

'Or just darn lucky!'

Trask was about to answer when he noticed that his gunbelt and pair of Eagle-Butt Colts were no longer hanging across the neck of his mount. His hands searched the golden mane of the stallion as if his eyes were lying to him.

They were not.

The holstered guns and the gunbelt were gone.

Suddenly he realized that they must have fallen off the neck of his stallion somewhere a dozen miles back when he and Waldo had forced their mounts to jump from the high ridge into the river. The gunfighter continued to stare at his horse's mane. But when did he lose them? The question taunted him as he tried to remember the events that he had tried so hard to forget. Blood dripped from his hair on to his hands and brought him back to reality.

He knew that he had been firing blindly at the Indians who had attacked them in the forest but when the Colt was empty, he had returned it to its holster and secured its hammer with the small leather safety loop.

From there his memory was vague.

'You looks like you seen a ghost, Trask,' Cooper noted as he took the weight of the mountain man on his broad shoulder. 'What's eatin' ya?'

Trask looked up at the pair of bearded men.

'My guns!'

'What about them?'

'They've gone!' Trask sighed heavily. 'I've lost my guns!'

Waldo Zane leaned on the equally large Cooper and stared hard at the gunfighter's face. He had seen the man face an Indian attack without a single hint of emotion and yet now the old-timer actually looked troubled.

'They must have fallen off ya hoss in that damn river back aways, Trask!' Waldo said. 'You're lucky that you're still alive. Hell! You and me both are lucky we're still alive. Don't go frettin' about no guns! You're still alive, that's all that counts!'

Trask dismounted and rested a hand on the saddle horn. 'But them were my guns. They were the guns of Trask.'

Waldo Zane turned and allowed Cooper to help him inside the trading post.

'Guns is guns!' Cooper chipped in.

'C'mon, old-timer,' the mountain man grunted. 'Josh'll sell ya as many guns as ya wants.'

Trask tied his reins next to those of the grey. He rubbed the blood from his face and swallowed hard. For the first time in his entire adult life he was without the famed weaponry. What if he had been right all the years that he had worn them? What if it were the guns themselves that were somehow possessed by some magical power? Without them, he might not have a chance to outdraw anyone ever again.

'C'mon, Trask!' Waldo shouted from inside the trading post.

Trask exhaled and slowly trailed the large men inside the building. With every step, he wondered how long he would last now that the guns had gone.

15

The small, agile, painted ponies beneath their masters showed little sign of the relentless chase they had just participated in. The Indians had searched vainly for their prey along the bank of the river for more than an hour after the brutal pursuit of Trask and Zane had ended.

They could find no trace of either horseman. Red Eagle looked down into the deep fast-flowing water from the high ridge where the two riders had crashed through the undergrowth and fallen at full gallop.

Even he could not imagine anyone surviving either the fall or the strong current. His hooded eyes had seen the white water a half-mile downriver, indicating the ragged rocks beneath the river's surface.

Red Eagle had no wish to continue

their search. Yet his was a lone voice amongst so many younger, angrier ones.

'The white men must have died,' he muttered. 'Their fear of us killed them. No rider could fall from here and live. Water too deep and fast. Rocks would strip the flesh from their bones. We go now back to our camp. We hunt and get fresh game for feasting. Red Eagle says they are dead!'

The warriors drew their ponies closer. They had not been satisfied with the chase that had seen one of their dwindling band die.

Wild Dog was less than half the age of Red Eagle but twice as loud and countless times more vicious. He had the scalps of more than fifty souls on his war lance and craved even more. He clenched his fist and waved it under the nose of the older warrior.

'You are a woman, Red Eagle. You would sit down and die of old age if it were not for us. We are the last braves of our tribe. We did not ask to be slaughtered like buffalo. We have nothing left to do except to kill the invaders.'

'But we are the invaders of this land, Wild Dog.' Red Eagle corrected the blood-crazed youth. 'This is the land of the Cheyenne and others. The bearded ones have been here before any of us were even born. To kill a true enemy is good but to just kill will make our gods angry!'

'What gods? Where are our gods? They deserted us long ago back on the plains. Where were they when our women and children and old ones were killed? We have no gods!'

Red Eagle lowered his head and stared at the water far below them. The cloudy sky made everything seem as grey as his broken soul felt.

'The men we sought are down there. They and their horses have drowned like all things drown in such places. What is it we shall hunt and kill now? Tell me, Wild Dog! Who shall we kill now?'

The face of Wild Dog burned with anger.

'We shall kill more of the white trappers!'

'Have you not killed enough of the bearded ones?' Red Eagle sighed as a few rays of sunshine flickered through the angry sky above the forest.

'We shall keep killing until we are no more!' Wild Dog snarled. 'We owe this to our people!'

'We owe them nothing but our prayers!' Red Eagle said.

Wild Dog pushed the barrel of his rifle into the face of the older brave.

'I should kill you. You are a woman.'

Red Eagle showed no fear.

'Kill me, Wild Dog. It would be a mercy for me to go to the Great Spirit.'

'The trading post!' Wild Dog lowered the rifle. 'We shall attack the trading post!'

The rest of the Indians started to chant as they thought about the well-stocked trading post.

'We should go hunt,' Red Eagle said

again. 'Catch fine deer and make feast!'

'There is plenty fire-water and food at trading post, old woman!' Wild Dog shouted. 'And many guns and bullets just waiting for us to take. I say we attack the trading post.'

The rest of the warriors all whooped their agreement until the forest echoed to their haunting tones.

'Come! We go!' Wild Dog turned his pony and kicked hard. The rest of the Indians galloped after the warrior up into the dark trees. Red Eagle remained at the ridge and watched as sunlight filtered through the branches all around him.

Red Eagle was about to turn his painted pony and follow the screaming warriors when something caught his eye. He pulled back on the black-and-white mane of the pony and gripped its body with his knees. He stared into the broken brush and up into the branches. At first the wisest of his people could not believe his eyes. He wondered why the other braves had not seen it hanging above the sheer drop over the river.

The dying rays of the afternoon sun cut through the trees above him. It was brighter now than it had been for the previous few hours.

The golden light danced on silver gun hammers.

His hooded eyes focused on the magnificent gunbelt suspended in mid air amid the leaves and broken twigs. Its pair of pearl-handled gun grips were still secured in their holsters.

The Indian felt as if he were a moth being lured to the light of naked flame. He tapped his feet against the sides of his pinto pony and urged it towards the steep edge of the high embankment.

The pony began to snort fearfully.

Red Eagle tried to force his mount closer but its unshod hoofs felt the soft yielding ground beneath it and shied away.

His outstretched right arm vainly tried to grab at the tempting gunbelt, but it was too far away. The warrior then recalled the repeating rifle that hung around his neck by a few thin feet of braided rawhide. He pulled the rifle over his head and then held on to its metal barrel. The warrior tried to hook its wooden stock under the middle of the swaying gunbelt.

Yet the further he leaned over with the long rifle in his hand, the less he seemed to be able to control the heavy weapon. Red Eagle summoned every ounce of his strength for one last attempt at capturing the alluring object.

'You shall not belittle Red Eagle as the young bucks of my tribe do,' the Indian brave whispered. 'I was once a great warrior who led his people to hunt the buffalo. You shall be mine, gleaming guns. You shall show the young bucks that I am the true leader of my people. When Red Eagle has you strapped around his middle, Wild Dog will not dare call me names again. Come to me, gleaming guns!'

Red Eagle took a firm hold of the pony's mane with his left hand and then teased the branches which held

Trask's famed gunbelt with his Winchester. The wooden stock pushed and knocked it until he could see the weight of the Colts drag down through the broken branches. Leaves floated down into the darkness of the river below him.

At last the gunbelt also fell.

Red Eagle caught the thick leather spine of it on the wooden stock of his rifle. He had never imagined that anything so beautiful could be so heavy. For a few seconds it balanced until its sheer weight forced the rifle in his outstretched hand to dip.

To his horror he could do nothing but watch as it slid off and fell.

'No!' Red Eagle cried as his pony stumbled. The brave fought to regain control of the terrified animal as its hoofs slid in the mud closer to the perilous edge of the ridge.

The aged brave strained every muscle in his aching body, trying not to follow the gunbelt and weapons down into the dark void below him. He dragged the head of the pony hard to his right and kicked at its ribs. At last he steadied the pinto and then heard the sound of the splash from his high vantage point.

Before he could do another thing, he heard the voice of Wild Dog calling out through the trees behind him.

'Are you coming, old woman?'

The warrior dragged the head of the painted pinto around and kicked the animal hard. He galloped towards the mocking voice.

16

There was an unseen force that dragged the outlaw on and on like a puppet-master toying with his helpless marionette. Pate Davis had spotted the churned-up ground which had been carved across the dirt-track trail a few hours earlier when he and his five riders had gone in vain search of the gun battle they had heard echoing through the forest. Now he was helpless to do anything except keep following the trail. Vengeance was a cruel master and he its more than willing servant.

No tracker could have followed the trail of shod and unshod hoof-prints any better. Davis steered his mount between the trees with his five nervous followers never more than a few yards behind him.

It was as if Davis ignored the warning signs which were everywhere. The countless bullet-scarred tree trunks did not deter or slow him as he continued to spur on and on.

The outlaw was deaf to the men who protested behind him for him to stop.

He was oblivious to the dangers that they knew were getting closer with every stride of their horses.

For Pate Davis had only one thing in his fevered brain. It was catching up with the mysterious Trask and dishing out his own brand of vengeance.

At last Strother Jackson could no longer keep his fear to himself. He whipped his long reins across the shoulders of his lathered-up mount and rode to the side of the silent outlaw.

'Pate!' he snapped loudly. 'Rein in, Pate. We gotta talk!'

Davis glanced to his side. His eyes burned into Jackson before he pulled back on his reins and stopped the horse beneath him.

'What ya want, Strother?'

Jackson gulped hard.

'You're trailin' Injuns, Pate! A whole

bunch of them by the looks of it, and me and the boys don't wanna ride into any trouble with their sort! Catchin' and killin' an old-timer like Trask is one thing, but none of us got any hankerin' to tangle with no gun-happy Injuns!'

Davis fumbled in his coat-pocket and found a cigar. He carefully broke it into two and pocketed one half whilst putting the other in his mouth.

'I'm trailin' Trask!' he muttered as his thumbnail ignited a match. He held the flame beneath the cigar and sucked hard on the strong smoke.

Jackson pointed at the ground and then all about them.

'And Injuns, Pate! Look at the ground! Unshod hoof-tracks. You're trackin' a whole pack of them!'

'Reckon?'

'Yep, I reckon.' Jackson nodded. 'Look at the trees. They're shot up real good. Seems to us that these Injuns got themselves a lot of rifles and they ain't feared of usin' them!'

'How can ya be certain that it's

Injuns?' Davis asked as smoke billowed from his gritted teeth. 'The ground is so churned up it could be shod horses for all we know.'

Strother Jackson looked over his shoulder at the four other riders. He indicated with a flick of his head for Luke Parsons to join them.

'Come show Pate what ya plucked off them bushes a few miles back, Luke!'

Parsons tapped his spurs and rode to the other side of the outlaw. He handed the long eagle-feather with red paint on its tip to Davis.

Davis held the feather and stared at it hard.

'Where'd ya find this?'

Parsons pointed behind them.

'Back there. Ya rode straight past it. Ya was lookin' so hard at the ground, ya never even seen the darn thing!'

Davis sucked hard on the cigar and then handed the feather back to the nervous rider beside him. His eyes darted back at Jackson.

'OK! So we're trailin' Injuns! So what?'

Jackson swallowed hard.

'Ya think that we can tussle with Injuns, Pate?'

Davis nodded slowly.

'Yep! C'mon!'

The five horsemen watched as Davis spurred his horse and continued to follow the trail down through the tall pines and broken brush.

The five riders had an easy choice to make. They either rode on and possibly ran into Indians or they could risk the wrath of Davis.

Silently they spurred and trailed the outlaw. Then, less than a hundred yards further along the uneven ground, they noticed Davis slow his mount, stand in his stirrups and look to his right.

'What's wrong, Pate? What ya seen?' Jackson asked as he drew in his reins.

Davis did not reply. He dragged his horse to where he was looking and then allowed it to descend the steep muddy slope towards the river.

The last rays of sunlight danced over the surface of the rippling water, highlighting everything on the riverbed beneath its cold liquid.

All five horsemen followed Davis like sheep trailing a ram. None of them was either willing or able to ask more questions. It was clear that Davis's sharp gunfighter eyesight had spotted something just beneath the surface of the water close to the riverbank.

But what?

They watched curiously as the outlaw looped his reins around his saddle horn and quickly dismounted. Jackson grabbed at the bridle of the outlaw's horse and steadied it as the lean figure walked into the fast-flowing river until his high-heeled boots were submerged in its water.

Davis waded out until the ice-cold water was above the sides of his boots. He leaned down, pushed his arm into the river and fished the gunbelt out of its watery resting-place.

'Damn! Look what I found, boys!'

Pate Davis said triumphantly as he screwed up his eyes and stared at the unique belt and its silver guns held in place by the small leather safety loops over the hammers.

'Pate must have eyes like a hawk!' one of the riders muttered under his breath.

'Them guns must have bin in that river for years. They'll be all rusted up by now, Pate,' Parsons said. 'Ya might as well toss them back in!'

'They don't look very rusty to me.' One of the horsemen disagreed as the sunlight glanced across the silver gun grips and pearl-handled inlays.

'They ain't!' The outlaw walked back out of the river and then held the heavy gunbelt in both hands. He read the name that was branded into its leather.

A look of utter disbelief etched his hardened features.

'Trask! These guns ain't been wallowing in this water long, boys. They're darn fresh. They're the guns that killed Denver Ben! They're the guns of Trask!'

The riders all gasped.

'Can't be!' exclaimed Parsons. 'Ain't possible.'

'His name is branded on the belt!' Davis snapped back. 'I don't reckon that there could be two back-shootin' varmints both called Trask!'

A stunned Strother Jackson jumped from his horse and moved to the outlaw. He read the name for himself.

'Sure enough, it says Trask all right, boys!' he confirmed. Parsons looked at the open-mouthed faces of the other riders before returning his attention to Davis holding the gunbelt.

'What the hell was it doing in there?'

Strother Jackson moved closer to the outlaw.

'Maybe them Injuns killed Trask and tossed him and his gunbelt into the river, Pate! Maybe the old-timer is dead! Maybe we ought to head on back to Hickory!'

'I figure Strother's right.' Parsons nodded from atop his mount. 'You're chasin' a ghost, Pate. Ain't nothin' but loco to keep chasin' a dead man.'

Fury welled up inside the outlaw. Davis sucked on his cigar, pulled one of Trask's silver Colts from its holster and cocked its hammer. He aimed the deadly weapon at Luke Parsons and grinned through the smoke that trailed from his mouth.

'Loco am I? *Adios*, Luke!' Davis squeezed the trigger of the weapon. Its wet hammer fell, but nothing happened. The outlaw repeated the action five more times and then pushed the gun back into its holster. Then he drew the other of Trask's infamous guns and cocked it. Again the Colt refused to fire like its identical twin.

Pate Davis spat the cigar at the ground and grunted with disappointment. He angrily pushed the Colt back into its holster and threw Trask's gunbelt over his horse's neck. He mounted and looked at the shaking Parsons. He laughed.

'You're a mighty lucky man, Luke. I bet that's the first time anyone ever lived after having either of these guns aimed at 'em. Reckon they don't like gettin' wet! That's the trouble with damn Colts, that's why I use Remingtons.'

Parsons blinked hard and said nothing. He knew the deadly outlaw was correct. Somehow he had survived having both the guns of Trask aimed and fired at him.

Jackson stepped into his stirrup.

'What we doin' now, Pate?'

'We're gonna carry on following that trail up there,' Davis said. He turned the horse and spurred hard. The animal went up the muddy slope until it was back on the higher ground. 'I still got me a gut feelin' that old Trask is still livin'. If he is, I intend stopping him do that!'

Cautiously, Strother Jackson looked at the four other horsemen.

'C'mon, boys,' he whispered, 'we don't wanna make him draw them Remingtons of his, do we? They're dry and mean just like their master!'

The five riders whipped their horses into action and rode after the outlaw.

17

The coal-oil in the half-dozen lanterns
dotted around the interior of the
trading post made a lot of black smoke
which drifted up to the wooden-
beamed ceiling. Trask could taste it in
the back of his throat as he stared into
the tin cup containing a mixture of
whiskey and coffee. The cup had been
hot when Josh Cooper had given it to
him but now was as cold as the air
which circulated around the large
buildings made of logs.

Waldo Zane was even more remark-
able than Trask had first thought. When
he had removed the large fur coat from
his massive frame, three neat bullet
holes in his broad meaty back were
revealed.

Yet Zane had dismissed the injuries
as if they were nothing more than
annoying bee-stings and refused to

allow Cooper to try and dig out the lead bullets from his flesh.

Trask had noted that the big man had a lot of similar scars on his body. Apart from tell-tale signs that the holes had been sewn up, there were no signs that he had ever allowed anyone to attempt to remove the lead.

Waldo had already consumed a full bottle of whiskey before the sun had set. He was now looking at what remained of the second bottle's contents knowingly.

'How can you drink so much without getting drunk, Waldo?' Trask asked as he watched the half-naked man sit down on a flour-sack opposite him near the stove.

'I am drunk, Trask.' Waldo smiled as he held the bottle up and then poured it over his back. His teeth gritted as the hard liquor burned into the still fresh wounds.

Trask swilled the coffee and whiskey around in the tin cup before downing it. His eyes closed when the sheer strength of the whiskey burned its way down into his innards.

'Good stuff?' Cooper asked as he handed two plates into the hands of his visitors.

Trask looked at the huge lumps of cheese and piles of crackers on their plates. He then looked up at Cooper.

'Smooth. Real smooth,' he lied.

'Want another shot?'

'No thanks. But I could use a cup of straight black coffee.'

Joshua Cooper shrugged.

'Just coffee? Ain't never seen anyone drink the stuff neat before. But then ya are kinda older than most of the folks who come trading here.'

Trask balanced the plate on his knees and then pulled some cheese off the large chunk. It tasted good.

'How many folks live here?'

Cooper poured more coffee into the tin cup.

'Only me on a regular basis. I own the cabins and rent them out to the trappers when they come off the mountains. Nobody lives here all the time any more. Just me.'

Trask chewed and looked around at the wares.

'You sure got a lot of stock here.'

Cooper rested down on a soft sack next to Zane and bit off a plug of tobacco. He started to chew.

'Too much stock, Trask. I ought to be almost out of everything by now. Trouble is I seem to have lost most of my regular customers this year.'

Trask leaned forward.

'What you mean by 'lost', Josh?'

Cooper shrugged.

'The ornery varmints just ain't come out of the forests this summer.'

'Sounds a tad suspicious to me, Josh,' Trask said. 'Me and Waldo ran into a real vicious bunch of Indians up in them trees and they was hunting scalps.'

'I heard tales about them.' Cooper nodded. 'Do ya think they might have killed the trappers?'

'They was sure tryin' to kill me and

Trask!' Waldo said bluntly. 'I don't see why they'd shy away from trappers on their lonesome, Josh.'

Cooper felt a cold shiver trace his spine. He rose to go and close the sturdy door when he realized it was already closed and locked up tight.

'What's wrong, Josh?' Waldo asked as he placed the empty bottle on the floor next to him.

Cooper stood.

'Ya hear anythin' outside?'

'Nope,' Trask replied.

'Ya hearin' things, Josh. Sit down,' Zane said.

Joshua Cooper frowned.

'I'm sure I heard somethin' out there.'

Both seated men watched as a curious Cooper walked to the glass-panelled door.

Suddenly they heard the muffled sound of rifle shots. The glass in the door shattered into a thousand slivers. The hefty Joshua Cooper was lifted off the ground and fell backward. The ground shook when his lifeless body landed at the feet of his two startled guests.

Trask dropped his plate as he rose. 'Guns! Where are the guns?'

18

There is a breed of madness which comes from grief and total despair. It festers and grows like a cancer in the most sane of souls. It destroys all reason and turns its victims into murderous creatures with no humanity left in the void which once held their souls. This madness has no boundaries or limits to its destructive depravity. It destroys without even a hint of guilt or conscience.

It is probably the most dangerous and unpredictable of all its kind and can infect men and women of all colours and creeds alike. So it was with the Indians who surrounded Red Eagle on the banks of the Bighorn River as they watched Wild Dog empty his Winchester into the brightly illuminated trading post. To them, there was nothing left except to kill.

The crazed Wild Dog had fired the entire magazine of his rifle at the trading post to signal the start of his attack. He had no idea whether any of his well-grouped shots had hit anyone within the building.

He did not care either way.

When the smoking rifle was empty, he tossed the Winchester to one of the other braves to be reloaded.

'This is wrong, Wild Dog!' Red Eagle protested, grabbing at the younger brave's arm and pulling him around to face him. 'The Great Spirit will curse us for fighting during the hours of darkness. It is not permitted. For souls cannot find their gods until the sun has risen. You know this.'

Wild Dog pulled himself free, clenched both fists and then hit Red Eagle with all his strength. The brave fell into the swaying grass, stunned by the sheer power of the furious well-aimed blows.

'Taste your own blood, old woman.' Wild Dog laughed as he strode around the fallen elder. 'Do the gods make the pain less if you are a believer?'

Red Eagle twisted around and then rose again to his feet.

'You are strong with youth but evil has soured your mind to all things which make a man. Think on, Wild Dog. There is a whole life ahead of you should you wish to find it. This course takes you to almost certain destruction.'

'All things die!' Wild Dog sneered. 'I choose to die fighting our enemies. You would let them take everything and then thank them for doing so.'

Red Eagle strode toward the furious young buck.

'You are mad!'

Wild Dog leapt.

His powerful fingers encircled the throat of the older warrior. Red Eagle could feel his neck being crushed mercilessly by the vicious brave.

Somehow Red Eagle managed to push both his own hands up between the arms of his crazed attacker. He forced the hands away from his throat and then kicked Wild Dog's legs from under him.

As he fell he reached out and grabbed at Red Eagle's legs. The older Indian felt himself toppling. Both men rolled down the grassy embankment and into the ice-cold river.

The rest of the excitable braves started to whoop as they watched the hand-to-hand combat below them. Water splashed up into the bright moonlight as one of the soaked Indians clawed his way up out of the water.

At first it was not clear who was trying to get back on dry land. Then it became clear that it was Wild Dog. The Indian shook his long mane of hair until he could see Red Eagle staggering after him.

He kicked out and caught the chin of the panting brave. Red Eagle fell back. The splash sent water over the chanting onlookers.

'Kill the old woman, Wild Dog!' a voice from behind the young buck encouraged.

Wild Dog grabbed a tomahawk from one of the other Indians and took aim. As the bedraggled warrior surfaced and started towards him yet again, he threw it.

The glancing blow caught Red Eagle high on his head. With blood tracing down his wet features, he staggered, yet continued towards the enraged brave.

Again Wild Dog threw his entire weight into the older man. They crashed at the feet of the others and clawed at each other with their bare hands. Then Red Eagle somehow managed to get back on his feet. He clenched his right fist and hit Wild Dog with such force that the young brave went head over heels.

Wild Dog spat blood from his mouth and laughed.

'You even hit like a woman!' he mocked. The younger Indian did not seem to feel any pain. He merely moved faster and struck out harder.

A punch to the stomach and another to the head sent Red Eagle crashing to the ground again.

'Stay there, old woman!' Wild Dog commanded. 'I have had enough of you. We have all had enough of you and your words. You are not our chief. Our chief is dead.'

Red Eagle refused to remain on the ground. He spat the blood from his mouth and then drew himself back up on to his knees and then to his full height once again.

'Is it the sanity of my words that frightens you, Wild Dog? Are you afraid to listen in case I say something that will haunt you until the day you perish?'

Wild Dog screamed. It was the most chilling of sounds.

Red Eagle saw Wild Dog throw the knife a second before it sliced through the right sleeve of his heavy buckskin jacket. The pain stopped him in his tracks. Then a two-fisted blow forced him backwards into the grass once more. He lay for a few moments until his eyes cleared and then forced himself back on to his knees.

'Look at him, my brothers!' Wild Dog yelled, pointing. 'I think it is Red Eagle who is crazed, not I. Only one who is insane would keep returning to be punished.'

'I am not afraid of you, young one!' Red Eagle said as blood flowed from his wounds.

Wild Dog moved closer to his audience and accepted another razor-sharp knife from one of the chanting braves. He ran a thumbnail along its honed edge and then leapt like a panther at the dazed warrior.

With one swift action, Wild Dog grabbed the hair of his opponent, jerked his head back and placed the gleaming blade against the throat of the bleeding Red Eagle.

'I should kill you now, old woman!' Wild Dog snarled into the ear of his weakened victim. 'Your scalp would look good on my war lance.'

Red Eagle still showed no fear.

'Then you will never find your place

in the Happy Hunting Grounds with the rest of your family, Wild Dog. You shall wander eternity neither alive or dead if you betray the wishes of the gods!'

The words confused Wild Dog. He released his grip and kicked the older man hard enough to make him roll over on to his back.

'Don't you understand? Our gods have abandoned us!' he shouted as his reloaded rifle was returned to him. 'We are already doomed by the white eyes. They have taken away everything: our lives and even our deaths. All we can do is to try and kill as many of them as we can now.'

Red Eagle propped himself up on his elbows and looked up at the crazed youth.

'I pity you, Wild Dog! I have lost more than any of you but I do not hate. For hatred only destroys he who hates.'

'Fool!' Wild Dog pushed the magazine lever down and then pulled it back up until the rifle was primed. He rested its wooden stock on his thigh and then squeezed the trigger. The noise was deafening.

Red Eagle's prostrate body shook as the bullet hit him dead centre.

Even in the light of the moon the droplets of blood could be seen as they splattered out of the old Indian warrior. Red Eagle gave a groan and fell back into the grass.

'Now we attack the white eyes, my brothers!'

The braves started to make their way on foot towards the array of log cabins. With each step they took, they fired their deadly rifles into the heart of the main building.

★　★　★

At first it had sounded as if a thunderstorm was unleashing its venom up the valley toward Cooper's Point. Then every one of the cavalry-men realized that it was not the clear moonlit sky that created the chilling sounds. It was men with rifles in their hands.

It was as if every one of the fifty troopers stood up at exactly the same moment from the small camp-fire they had made a few miles south of Cooper's Point. Colonel John Edison threw his tin cup at the ground and then ran to the side of the burly sergeant.

'Hear those shots, Brewster?'

'A deaf man could have heard 'em, sir! Sounds like all hell broke loose up at the trading post!'

Edison looked at the faces illuminated in the flickering light of the fire until he located O'Hara.

'Get the men to saddle up their horses at the double, Captain!' he ordered.

O'Hara saluted and began to usher the stunned cavalrymen toward their horses.

'You heard the colonel, men. Saddle up.'

Colonel Edison gritted his teeth.

'The next time I suggest we make camp a few miles from our destination, Brewster, you have my permission to kick my blistered backside! What possessed me? I must be getting old.'

Sergeant Brewster lifted both their saddles off the ground and handed one to colonel.

'I'd love to oblige but I reckon we ought to get our nags readied real quick, sir.'

Edison placed the blanket on top of the charge's back and patted it down before throwing his saddle over it. As he reached under the belly of the muscular horse, the officer listened as the sounds of shooting away off in the distance started up again. He had heard the same noise many times during his long existence but had never grown used to it.

'Who on earth do you think is fighting, Brewster?'

Sergeant Brewster tightened his cinch strap and hurriedly pulled the stirrups down. He looked round to check that their troopers were starting to mount.

'Do ya think it might be them Injuns we keep hearing tales about, sir?'

'Indians attacking at night?' Colonel Edison felt his throat tighten. 'Is that possible? I always thought that all the tribes had some sort of religious reason for not fighting when the sun was set.'

'If it is Injuns maybe they've lost their faith in their gods, sir!' Brewster suggested.

The colonel mounted and gathered up his loose reins.

'Indians who have rejected their gods? I sure hope that you are wrong, Brewster.'

'Why?'

Edison turned the powerful horse.

'Why? Because sometimes that's the only advantage we have against them.'

Both men's attention was drawn to the gelded chestnut that trotted up to them. Captain O'Hara stopped his mount next to the charger and saluted.

'The men are ready, sir.'

Edison returned the salute before he

glanced towards Brewster and nodded.

Sergeant Brewster understood the unspoken command. He raised an arm and shouted at the top of his voice.

'Forward ho!'

The fifty-one horsemen headed into the night towards the distant trading post at full gallop. They carved a direct route through the swaying moonlit grass, leaving the flames of their campfire far behind them.

19

The chilling Indian war cries mixed with the deafening rifle shots as Wild Dog and his warriors mercilessly bore down on the trading post. There was little left of the building's front door as the dozens of Winchesters continued to level their fury into the centre of the solid structure.

The acrid stench of gunsmoke filled the nostrils of the two men trapped inside. After Joshua Cooper had been cut down by the first of the rifle shots, Trask had extinguished all the store's lanterns in a desperate hope that their attackers would not shoot at targets they could no longer see.

The gunfighter had been wrong.

The rifle bullets had continued to tear into the trading post with increased ferocity. Glass and sawdust covered everything within the building as Trask tried to load the brand-new guns Waldo Zane had found for him in Cooper's shattered display cabinet.

'Ain't ya gonna shoot back, Trask?' the mountain man asked as he tried to protect his impressive bulk from the bullets that continued to rain down on them.

'These guns ain't ever been fired before, Waldo,' Trask replied. 'They need oilin'.'

'Just shoot the darn things, old-timer!' Waldo snorted. 'Try and kill them before they ups and kills us.'

'First I gotta get near the door. Even I can't kill somethin' I can't see.' Trask closed the chambers of the guns and swallowed hard. Bullets ripped into barrels and shelves all around them. 'But getting there ain't as easy as it sounds.'

'They'll storm us at any moment.' Zane cradled a shotgun in his lap and emptied a cardboard box of shells on to the floor beside him. He slid two of the red-and-gold cartridges into the large chambers of the gun and snapped it shut.

Trask looked at the unfamiliar weapons in his hands, then nodded silently to himself. He had to act and act soon. No matter how many bullets were pinning him and the mountain man down, he had to try and stop the Indians.

He had to try and forget that he no longer had Trask's magnificent guns to protect him. The veteran gunfighter had to try and make the pair of new ones do his bidding.

The moonlight was bright on the front of the trading post. He screwed his eyes up and watched as more rifle bullets ripped what was left of the door off its hinges. It fell, sending a cloud of dust up into the eerie blue air.

'You any good at loading six-shooters, Waldo?' Trask asked as he hovered on his boots waiting for a lull in the shooting so that he could run to the front wall next to the gaping hole where the door had once stood. 'I reckon I could give as good as I took if'n there was someone loading my guns for me.'

Waldo Zane held out his huge hands and displayed his thick fingers.

'Are ya joshin'? Me stick li'l bullets in them li'l holes in them li'l guns?'

Trask had never seen such large fingers before. He could have placed his own hand in the palm of the trapper's with the fingers outstretched.

'Guess not. No wonder you use that buffalo gun.'

Zane clenched his fist and thumped the floor angrily.

'Tarnation! I just remembered that I left my old buffalo gun on Curly's saddle in the corral!'

Suddenly there was a pause in the rifle fire. Trask cocked the hammer of one of the guns and pushed the other into his pants' belt. He picked up the box of .45 bullets and then gritted his teeth.

'Here goes!'

Zane watched the older man race

across the room dodging stray bullets towards the wall made of solid timbers.

Trask threw himself on to floor and rolled over the slivers of shattered glass and splintered remnants of the door until he hit the wall. The gunfighter felt a sharp pain in his side and instinctively knew he had burst the stitches. He could feel his warm blood trace its way down his side.

'You OK, Trask?' Zane shouted as he moved between the stacks of large boxes towards the shattered window on the front wall.

Trask cleared his throat.

'Yep!' he lied.

'Then shoot the varmints, ya old fool!'

Trask licked his lips and looked around the corner of the splintered doorframe. He could see their attackers moving through the swaying grass less than thirty feet from where he knelt.

'I see the critters!' he said.

'Then kill 'em, Trask!' Zane called out as he reached the window and rested against the wall. 'Must be the same sidewinders as tried to snuff us out up in the trees. Let's see some of that fancy gunfightin' shootin'.'

Trask narrowed his eyes and focused. He fanned the gun hammer and watched as his bullets cut through the darkness at the warriors. Blinding gunsmoke hung on the cold air a few yards from the barrel of the Colt. He could not tell how many of his shots had found their mark as another volley of bullets came at him from all directions.

Trask dropped on to the floor as hot lead cut through the air a few inches above him.

'How many did ya kill, old-timer?' Waldo Zane shouted.

'Not enough by the sound of it!' Trask lay on his belly and cocked the hammer of the other gun. He could just make out the shapes of the warriors as they moved swiftly through the swaying grass.

He fired.

A muffled cry reached his ears.

Waldo Zane inhaled and used the wooden stock of his shotgun to break what was left of the window panes before he pointed the double-barrelled weapon out of the window and squeezed both the large triggers.

Even at ten yards the buckshot was deadly.

The blast knocked the mountain man's muscular shoulder back a few inches. He discharged the two empty casings and clumsily pushed two more shells into the hot chambers.

He snapped the shotgun back together and pushed its barrel out of the window for a second time.

'Ya should have plucked up one of these scatterguns, Trask!' Zane called out. 'Better than them pea-shooters you got.'

Trask fired again and saw an Indian fall. He was about to reply when he heard the large man groan. It was the most horrific noise he had ever heard. Trask quickly rolled over again and stood up on the other side of the door frame. He looked over the piles of goods towards the window.

His eyes narrowed as he saw the mountain man leaning on the wall shaking.

'Waldo?' Trask called out.

Zane dropped the shotgun and then turned towards the gunfighter. He hovered like a tree waiting to fall after having its roots severed. Trask could see the blood pouring from the hole in the middle of the man's massive chest.

Then he fell.

Trask tucked both Colts into his belt, then leapt over every obstacle between them until he reached Zane. He dropped on to his knees beside the stricken mountain man and stared at the blood pumping from the middle of the man's chest. He lifted the bearded head up and rested it on his knees.

'The trouble with you mountain men is that you're too big to get out of the way of bullets.' Trask sighed. 'This looks bad, Waldo! Darn bad!'

'It's just a scratch, old-timer!' Waldo said. 'I've had me a lot worse than this.'

Before Trask could respond he felt the massive man shudder in his arms. The bearded face fell limply to the side. Waldo Zane was gone.

Trask gently lowered the head on to the ground and plucked up the shotgun and box of shells. He rose and snorted angrily as he made his way back to the gaping hole in the front of the wall which had once been a door.

'You wanna fight, Indians? I'll give ya a damn fight!'

20

The haunting sound of the cavalry bugle stopped Trask dead in his tracks. He hovered by the doorway of the trading post with the cocked shotgun in his hands and pair of Colts tucked in his pants. The gunfighter suddenly noticed that although he could still hear the Indians' Winchesters being fired, they were no longer aimed in his direction.

Trask recognized that the bugle was playing the 'charge' and that could mean only one thing. The cavalry were closing in on Cooper's Point.

The fact that they were arriving too late to save the lives of the two burly men who lay on the floor of the trading post did nothing to hearten the sad gunfighter.

A noise drew Trask's honed instincts. Suddenly an Indian ran from the long grass towards the trading post with his rifle in his left hand. Trask pulled himself back and allowed the brave to race past him. He then brought the barrel of the heavy weapon down on the Indian's head with all his might. He heard the skull crack and watched in horror as the warrior fell lifelessly to the ground just inside the doorway next to the body of Joshua Cooper.

Trask peered out into the moonlight. He could see troopers falling from their mounts as the Indians fired their repeating rifles at the courageous cavalry.

He knew that he had to try and stop another slaughter.

Cautiously, Trask edged out on to the porch and deliberately avoided the moonlight. He moved into the shadows until he was behind the Indians.

Wild Dog and his followers were frantically firing their rifles at the approaching horsemen who were bearing down on them. Trask levelled the shotgun and blasted both barrels at the closest of the Indians.

At least half a dozen of the braves were torn apart by the vicious buckshot. What was left of them turned their weaponry on the gunfighter.

Trask moved to his left as a score of bullets ripped the wooden wall apart. His eyes were filled with burning sawdust as he reloaded the shotgun and fired once more.

The blast cut down another handful of the warriors.

Then he saw the painted face of Wild Dog as the crazed Indian ran at him with his rifle aimed straight at his middle.

Trask dropped the smoking shotgun and pulled both his Colts from his belt. He had no idea which of the weapons in his hands were still loaded. He squeezed both triggers and felt the gun in his left hand kick as it delivered the fatal bullet straight between the eyes of his attacker.

Wild Dog fell at the feet of the gunfighter. Realizing that both guns were now filled with only the brass casings of spent bullets, Trask shook the shells from both the six-shooters and then hauled bullets from his pockets and started to refill the hot smoking chambers of each of the weapons in turn.

Age had not slowed his speed at reloading his guns.

He flicked his wrists and used his thumbs to lock the cylinders before cocking both hammers. The entire operation had taken less than thirty precious seconds.

Trask was ready for action!

The Indians had exhausted most of their ammunition in their vain attempt to stop the troopers' relentless approach. They started to run towards the trading post, knowing that they would find thousands of rounds somewhere within its four walls.

Trask blasted one after another until the remaining braves turned tail and ran through the long grass back to where they had left their painted ponies near the Bighorn River and the body of Red Eagle.

Trask stood and watched as the troop of cavalry pulled up outside the trading post and Colonel Edison looked down at the gunfighter.

'Which way did the Indians go, sir?'

It was an exhausted Trask who pointed in the direction of the river and sighed.

'They went thataway, Colonel. Reckon they must have their mounts over near the river someplace.'

'You did a great job here,' Edison remarked as he steadied the charger. 'You've probably saved the lives of most of my men by your courage.'

Trask nodded.

Edison touched the brim of his hat.

'Thank you kindly, sir. C'mon men.' He pulled the charger's neck hard to his left and spurred him on. The troop galloped off in the direction of the river.

Soon the sound of shooting started again. This time it was the fleeing Indians who were the hunted and the cavalry the hunters.

But to the veteran gunfighter it all seemed so utterly pointless.

Slowly, Trask lowered the smoking guns and stared out into the moonlight. He could see the Indians on their painted ponies being pursued by the cavalrymen upriver. He watched until he could no longer see them, then turned and looked at the bodies that were all around him.

So many bodies.

Trask felt sick to his stomach. He turned angrily and threw both the guns as far as he could into the long grass. Then he sat down on the edge of the water-trough and cupped his face in the palms of his hands.

He had no idea how long he had remained in exactly the same spot but it must have been a long time. Then he heard birds starting to sing all around the scene of carnage.

Trask raised his head.

The moon and stars were gone and the sky had started to get lighter as a new day was about to begin. Trask exhaled heavily and got back to his feet.

Suddenly the ground next to his boots kicked up dust. Then he heard the sound of a gunshot echo across the valley floor.

The gunfighter tilted his head and looked past his shoulder. He stared at the six horsemen who were closing in on him.

Pate Davis held one of his Remingtons in his right hand as he led his companions towards the trading post.

'I'm lookin' for an old-timer named Trask!' Davis drawled.

Trask squared up to the approaching horsemen and rested his knuckles on his hips.

'You found him!'

Finale

Trask watched as the horsemen slowly approached. They circled him, then reined in. Pate Davis threw his right leg over his horse's neck and slid to the ground. He handed his reins to Strother Jackson and studied the veteran figure before him with blazing eyes.

'Who are you?' Trask asked, continuing to rest his knuckles defiantly on his hips.

Davis grinned and pulled the half-cigar from his coat pocket. He placed it carefully between his teeth. He pulled a match from his vest pocket and ran his thumbnail across its tip. He cupped the flame and sucked in the smoke.

'Who are you?' Trask repeated his question.

Davis exhaled and tossed the match away.

'I'm Denver Ben's brother, Trask.'

Trask raised an eyebrow as the first rays of sun spread across the fertile valley.

'So you're Pate Davis. I've heard of you.'

Davis gave a twisted smile.

'What ya heard, old-timer?'

'I heard that Denver Ben had a loco kid brother,' Trask said bluntly. 'Reckon you must be it.'

Davis lowered his head and then glanced at his five mounted companions. They were all silent.

'Looks like Trask has a real big mouth, boys!' he snarled. His hands pushed his coat over the grips of his holstered Remingtons. 'Maybe I should shoot the old critter here and now. What ya think, boys?'

Only Jackson had the nerve to speak.

'He ain't armed, Pate.'

Davis looked back at Trask.

'I never noticed. All I could see was the killer who gunned down Denver Ben.'

'Killin' an unarmed man ain't got no worth, Pate,' Jackson added. 'Folks will say that ya was afraid of him.'

Pate Davis raised his head and stared through the cigar smoke at the gunfighter before him.

'By the looks of all these dead Injuns scattered around here you must have had some guns a while back. Where are they?'

Trask gritted his teeth and glared at the outlaw.

'I threw them away.'

Davis laughed.

'You loco? Why would ya throw guns away?'

Trask shrugged.

'Reckon I just had me a gutful of killing, Davis.'

The outlaw removed the cigar from his mouth and dropped it on the blood-stained ground at his feet. He pressed his right boot on to the smouldering butt and then took a step forward.

'How the hell did ya kill my brother, old-timer?'

Trask tilted his head.

'I ain't too sure. Denver Ben was fast. So fast he put a bullet through me before I cleared my holsters. Maybe I was just a tad more accurate.'

Davis seemed pleased that his brother had managed to hit the famous gunfighter with one of his shots.

'I'm faster than Denver Ben, Trask!'

The older man nodded.

'I heard talk to that effect. Some say that there ain't nobody faster than you with a pair of Remingtons.'

The outlaw grinned. It was the twisted grin of a man who liked flattery.

'I ought to kill ya now. Ya deserve it.'

'I can't do nothing to stop you, Davis.' Trask raised his hands. 'If'n you've a mind to kill me, then do it.'

Davis held his hands over the gun grips of his holstered weapons.

'Ya all heard him, boys. He told me to kill him.'

Strother Jackson cleared his throat and caught the outlaw's attention.

'Pate?'

Davis glanced to his side at the mounted man who had hold of his own horse. He looked at Jackson as the horseman patted the infamous guns hanging across the horse's neck.

'Ain't ya forgot about these?' Jackson asked.

Trask squinted at the five riders in a vain attempt to see what Jackson was patting.

'Damn it all.' Davis laughed. 'I did forget about them guns in their fancy shootin'-rig, Strother.'

'Ya ought to give Trask his guns, Pate.' Jackson winked as the outlaw reached up and pulled the gunbelt off the neck of his lathered-up mount.

Davis grinned. The belt and its pair of matched Colts were still as wet as when he had hauled them off the riverbed. They had not worked when he had tried to kill Luke Parsons and he had a feeling that they would not work now.

Trask watched the outlaw turn back to face him. He instantly recognized the gunbelt he held in his left hand.

'Are these your guns, Trask?' Davis asked, walking to within a dozen feet of the gunfighter.

'Yep!' Trask replied. 'They're my guns. How did you get them, Davis?'

Davis tossed them into the hands of the older man.

'I went fishin', Trask.'

Trask could feel the water dripping between his fingers as he looked at the belt. He wondered how wet the Colts were in their hand-crafted holsters. He knew that if they were too wet they might not work and that would explain why Davis had given them to him.

'Strap 'em on!' Davis ordered. 'Strap 'em on and let's see how fast ya really are.'

Trask sighed heavily. He knew that the outlaw would not settle for anything less than a showdown. He looped the belt around his hips and buckled it up.

'Mind if I check to see if they're loaded?' Trask asked.

'Don't ya trust me?' Davis smiled.

'Nope!'

Davis returned his own hands to just above the grips of his Remingtons, then nodded.

'Check 'em, old-timer.'

Trask pulled one of the weapons from its holster and opened its chamber. It was loaded but was also full of water. He closed the gun and returned it to its holster.

'Ain't ya gonna check the other one?' Davis enquired.

'Reckon it's a tad damp, just like its brother,' Trask said. He squared up to the outlaw. 'I got me a gut feeling that there's a good chance neither of them will work. What do you reckon, Davis?'

Pate Davis's eyes narrowed. The smile evaporated.

'Draw!' he shouted.

A split second later, the five riders watched open-mouthed as both men went for their guns. Pate Davis cleared his holsters at exactly the same time as Trask.

They squeezed the triggers of their weapons.

Gunsmoke erupted from the four barrels and masked the distance between them. As the cold autumn breeze drifted across the valley and cleared the acrid smoke from Cooper's Point both men were still standing.

'They worked!' Davis gasped as he looked at the stunned horsemen. 'His damn guns worked!'

Trask watched as the outlaw dropped both his smoking .45s and then stumbled on to his knees. Davis's eyes rolled up as he fell on to his face.

Strother Jackson dismounted and rushed to the outlaw's body, then he looked at the gunfighter. He was as surprised as Davis had been.

'I don't get it. Pate tried them guns of yours a few times on the ride here, Trask. They didn't work. They was too waterlogged.'

Trask felt a cold shiver trace his spine as the realization dawned on him that once again the guns of Trask had seemingly done the impossible. He slid the Colts back into their holsters and rubbed his face thoughtfully.

'Take him back to Hickory Creek,' Trask told the men. 'He's worth enough to keep you all in whiskey for a year.'

'Don't ya want the bounty, Trask?'

'Nope.' Trask lowered his head and then turned. He walked slowly and silently back into the trading post. He was looking for a shovel to bury two big men with.

We do hope that you have enjoyed reading this large print book.

Did you know that all of our titles are available for purchase?

We publish a wide range of high quality large print books including:
Romances, Mysteries, Classics
General Fiction
Non Fiction and Westerns

Special interest titles available in large print are:
The Little Oxford Dictionary
Music Book, Song Book
Hymn Book, Service Book

Also available from us courtesy of Oxford University Press:
Young Readers' Dictionary
(large print edition)
Young Readers' Thesaurus
(large print edition)

For further information or a free brochure, please contact us at:
Ulverscroft Large Print Books Ltd.,
The Green, Bradgate Road, Anstey,
Leicester, LE7 7FU, England.
Tel: (00 44) **0116 236 4325**
Fax: (00 44) **0116 234 0205**

THE HIGH COUNTRY YANKEE

Elliot Conway

Joel Garretson quit his job as Chief of Scouts to travel to Texas and claim his piece of land. He needed to forget the killings he had seen — and done — fighting the Sioux and the Crow in Montana . . . But he soon has to confront Texas *pistoleros* and then, aided by a bunch of ex-Missouri brush boys, he faces the task of rescuing two women held by *comancheros* in their stronghold . . . In the territory of the Llana Estacado, New Mexico, the violent blood-letting will commence . . .

BLADE LAW

Jack Reason

A silver necklet was all that was left to identify the body of the man McKee found dead in the mountains. The brutal murder was the work of Juan Darringo and his bandits who had made the mountain ranges their lair of robbery and death . . . However, identification of the dead man was to lead McKee back to the mountains accompanied by a man intent on retribution. Now, forced to pit their wits against the cruel terrain, they also find themselves the prey in a hunt that will have only one outcome.